THE SILVER CHARIOT KILLER

It's Christmas week in New York, and the frozen body of Cletus Berry, Hobart Lindsey's partner, has been found in a back alley alongside that of a known criminal. Was there a connection between the two men? This wouldn't normally be Lindsey's case, but when a man's partner is killed, he must do something about it. Now separated from Marvia Plum, Lindsey is on his own, and the body count is set to rise unless he can solve the mystery of the Silver Chariot . . .

RICHARD A. LUPOFF

THE SILVER CHARIOT KILLER

Complete and Unabridged

LINFORD
Leicester

First published in Great Britain

First Linford Edition
published 2016

Copyright © 1996 by Richard A. Lupoff

A catalogue record for this book is available
from the British Library.

ISBN 978–1–4448–3024–8

Published by
F. A. Thorpe (Publishing)
Anstey, Leicestershire

Set by Words & Graphics Ltd.
Anstey, Leicestershire
Printed and bound in Great Britain by
T. J. International Ltd., Padstow, Cornwall

This book is printed on acid-free paper

For Whitey, Congo, Mr. Jinx, Smokey, Lady, Pepper, Snoopy, Bonzo, Lucy, Magnum, Daisy, Ramona, and Mister Boris Peabody. Faithful friends, none of whom has ever read a word I wrote.

1

Berry was dead, to begin with. There is no doubt whatever about that. The register of his burial was signed by the clergyman, the clerk, the undertaker, and the chief mourner. Richelieu signed it. And Richelieu's name was good upon the 'net for anything he chose to put his hand to.

Old Berry was dead as a door-nail.

Lindsey closed the glossy in-flight magazine and slipped it into the pocket of the seat in front of him. Leave it to the airlines to revive Dickens for the Christmas issue. He looked out of the Plexiglas window at the the moonlit clouds beyond the big jetliner's wing.

Of course it wasn't Berry, it was Marley. And it wasn't Richelieu, it was Scrooge. And it wasn't the internet, it was the London Stock Exchange.

But Cletus Berry was dead, if not yet buried; dead as a door-nail. And Hobart

Lindsey was flying to New York, probably in time for Berry's funeral, and certainly in time to try and find out what had happened to him.

Berry had been his fellow employee at International Surety. They'd been roommates during the orientation seminar when both of them were selected for SPUDS, International Surety's Special Projects Unit, and Berry had helped Lindsey research a couple of tricky cases. They were friends, or as close to friends as their positions allowed them to be in the wonderful world of the modern corporation.

Reaching under his seat, Lindsey pulled out the carrying case with his company-issue laptop computer, then looked around for someone to take his empty coffee cup away. The flight attendants were decked out in Santa Claus hats, complementing their quasinaval uniforms. But at the moment there were no flight attendants near Lindsey's row. The passenger to his left, a seriously overweight teenager wearing a Denver Nuggets cap with the bill pointing backwards, had fallen asleep and was wheezing softly with each breath. There was no climbing over him, and Lindsey didn't want to shake him awake.

Finally Lindsey put the empty cup carefully on the cabin floor. He booted up the computer and opened the file on the murder of his friend.

There wasn't much there. Lindsey had showed up at the Special Projects Unit of International Surety in Denver as usual that morning. The air was sparkling, if cold. As Mondays went, this one looked pretty good. Lindsey was starting to feel more comfortable in his new assignment as Desmond Richelieu's deputy.

For once Mrs. Blomquist had motioned Lindsey straight into the director's office. And for once Richelieu hadn't been seated behind his desk. He had been pacing, and his salt-and-pepper hair had been in disarray. He shoved a piece of paper at Lindsey, a print of the morning report from International Surety's New York regional headquarters, designated in the corporate plan as Manhattan East.

Special Projects Unit — SPUDS

— acted like a private empire within International Surety, but every 'detached' SPUDS operative kept up a liaison with the local offices of the company. International Surety was as procedure-bound and as paper-heavy as any multinational, but SPUDS agents were freed from the usual corporate structure. They reported directly to Richelieu. The Director ran SPUDS the way his onetime mentor, J. Edgar Hoover, had run the Federal Bureau of Investigation. The FBI was Hoover's private empire inside the Department of Justice, and SPUDS was Desmond 'Ducky' Richelieu's private empire inside International Surety.

The toughest cases came to SPUDS, the weirdest cases, and the biggest cases. Hobart Lindsey had handled some of the best — or worst — of them, but now he was on his way to New York to take care of a matter that had rattled his boss's empire to its foundation. Cletus Berry had been found in an alley in Hell's Kitchen, the old New York slum to the west of the theater district and Times

Square. The word had come via KlameNet/Plus from Morris A. Zissler, assistant to the International Surety branch manager, Manhattan East.

Lindsey took the computer printout and hurried from Richelieu's imposing suite to his own modest office. He picked up a telephone and called Zissler for more details.

It had been a freezing December morning in New York. A sanitation worker had entered the alley to pick up a load of trash. He found Berry. He called the cops. By the time they arrived at the scene, the body had lain in the freezing sleet long enough that the coroner's technicians had to chip it out of the ice.

Not that Berry was alone. With him was one Frankie Fulton, familiarly known as 'FF,' in part because those were his initials, but mainly because he was a longtime petty criminal, unsuccessful gambler, and perennial gangster wanna-be. Early in his career, Frankie had tried to bluff his way to the biggest pot in the biggest poker game he'd ever been in. He was deep in the hole, betting on credit

— itself a rarity in Frankie's circles — and put his all on one five-card hand. When it came time to show, Frankie triumphantly produced a king, nine and eight and three of diamonds, with one corner of a red ten peeping out between the king and the nine. Frankie reached for the pot with one hand and for his hat with the other, happily crowing, 'Diamond flush.'

Unfortunately for Frankie, another player had two pairs, one of which was the tens of clubs and diamonds. Frankie escaped from that incident with his life, a very badly broken leg that when healed left him walking with a marked limp, and the permanent nickname 'FF.' Frankie 'Four Flusher' Fulton, too, had needed to be chipped out of the frozen slush. The two men were equally dead.

'How did they buy it?' Lindsey demanded.

'Shot.' Zissler hummed into the phone. 'And that's a little bit odd. Fulton was shot a lot.' He paused.

'Come on,' Lindsey urged, 'you've got to help me.'

'Well, kneecapped — shot in both knees. That must have hurt like hell. And he was shot in both hands, and in both arms, and finally through the heart.'

'And no one noticed?'

'It was sleeting hard last night. And in New York people don't get involved.'

'You mean nobody heard the shots?'

'Eleventh Avenue isn't a great neighborhood, Mr. Lindsey. I don't guess you know New York, do you?'

'No, I don't.'

'Well, even in good neighborhoods, people don't like to get involved. In Hell's Kitchen — well . . . ' He stopped speaking and hummed softly.

Lindsey wondered how much of Zissler's humming it would take to get on his nerves. 'You're telling me all about this Fulton person. What's our interest in him? Did he have a policy with IS?'

'No, Mr. Lindsey, but when two bodies are found together, both of them shot — you see? And the cops knew Frankie Fulton. When they found the bodies and found Cletus Berry's ID, they called International Surety. I talked to a

7

detective. She knew all about Frankie Fulton. She didn't know anything about Mr. Berry. She wanted to know about him. I couldn't tell her much. I knew the guy. I met him a couple of times. That was all.'

Lindsey said, 'You met him? Tell me about that.'

'Mr. Berry had his own office; he didn't like to work out of Manhattan East. He just wanted us to pay his bills, get him office supplies. Typical SPUDS bigshot. He rented this little place and put a computer and a futon and a microwave in it and made himself a little home away from home. I was up there a couple of times to deliver documents. Arrogant, too good to hang out with us peons. Whoops . . . ' Zissler paused.

Lindsey said, 'Never mind. What about Berry?'

'Uh, he was just shot twice. Small-caliber rounds, the detective said. Police don't have a lab report yet, but the detective told me the holes were small and there wasn't much bleeding; almost certainly .22s. That wouldn't be too noisy, either, not like a .45 or even a Police Special.'

Lindsey's free hand was shaking as he held the phone. 'Where was Berry hit?'

'Not nice,' Zissler said. 'One gut-shot. That's really nasty. You shoot somebody like that when you want him to take a long time dying and to suffer a lot. The detective told me that, see? And the other was through the head. Made a hole in his forehead. Must have stayed in his brain; no exit wound. The detective said that the bullet must have bounced around inside his skull and chopped his brain to pieces. Probably still in there. Probably the coroner will get it out. The detective told me that.'

Lindsey told Zissler he was coming to New York. Mrs. Blomquist would set up the trip from Denver, and would Zissler please make arrangements for him in New York. He took Zissler's extension, got the name and number of the detective in charge of the case, and hung up. Lindsey had jotted notes on a yellow pad as Zissler spoke. He transferred the key

9

information to his pocket organizer and slipped it into his jacket, then trotted back to Richelieu's office.

Richelieu had run a comb through his hair and was seated behind his desk. 'You're going.'

'Of course.'

'It's IS business.'

'It's SPUDS business.'

Richelieu looked up at Lindsey. 'You're after my job, aren't you?'

'No way.'

Lindsey went back to his own office and logged onto KlameNet/Plus. He used his SPUDS override code to get into Cletus Berry's personnel file. How well had he really known Berry? After that first training course in Denver they'd only met a couple more times, always at SPUDS refresher meetings and seminars.

But Lindsey had a feeling that if he left Cletus Berry's murder in the hands of the NYPD, odds were it would never be solved; and if he relied on Morris Zissler to handle the matter, the odds would be even worse.

The man seemed earnest enough; just not too bright, and slightly on the smug side. Not a promising combination.

* * *

Lindsey shut down the laptop and slid it into its case. The teenager in the Denver Nuggets cap had sagged against him. Trying to get out from under the teenager's weight, Lindsey squirmed. The kid twitched in his sleep, jumped, then climbed out of his seat and waddled up the aisle toward the toilet.

Lindsey pulled the in-flight magazine out of the pocket in front of him again and flipped through the pages. The abridged reprint of *A Christmas Carol* was illustrated in colorful scenes that made Dickens' London look a lot like the set of a Tim Burton movie.

Lindsey sighed and gave up on the magazine. There was always the folder illustrating evacuation routes to study. It was a marvel of graphic communication, aimed at getting a message to a multilingual audience.

Outside the 777's windows the December moon shone so brightly that it seemed to blaze. A cloud layer beneath the jet reflected the moonlight. Above the plane the black sky was dotted with stars. However, there was no sign of either Santa's sleigh or the Star of Bethlehem.

The captain's voice broke Lindsey's reverie. They would be landing at JFK in half an hour. The temperature was well below freezing, and sleet was falling in New York.

Lindsey slipped his International Surety credit card into the slot in front of him and made an air-to-ground telephone call.

Morris Zissler had agreed to pick him up at the airport. At least the man was good for that. Lindsey wondered what Zissler looked like. Based on the man's voice he expected a heavyset, middle-aged man in a brown suit and a worn, striped tie.

Coming out of the jetway, Lindsey was engulfed in a maelstrom of travelers and the families and friends who turned out to greet them. Half the greeters and half the travelers had brightly wrapped gifts in their hands. He spotted his seatmate, the massive teenager, waddling from the gate, a flight bag in his hand. A spectacular blonde, as tall as the kid in the baseball cap but easily 200 pounds lighter, flew into his arms, hugging him and planting kisses on his face. Lindsey blinked. Maybe the fat kid had something that Lindsey didn't know about.

By the time the crowd had thinned, Lindsey spotted the man he guessed was Morris Zissler. He was not disappointed. 'Zissler?' he said, approaching the man.

'Yes, sir. Mr. Lindsey? Oh, I see you've got one of those little potato badges in your buttonhole, just like Mr. Berry. Just call me Moe, Mr. Lindsey. Welcome to New York.'

Zissler helped Lindsey collect his baggage, insisting on carrying the heavy flight bag from the claim area to the parking lot. The sleet was falling and Lindsey turned up the collar of his seldom-used overcoat. He didn't have a hat, and he could feel his hair starting to crust over with sleet. Maybe the kid in the

Nuggets hat had been more on the ball than met the eye.

With a grunt that interrupted his humming, Zissler hefted Lindsey's flight bag into the trunk of a new sedan. Lindsey held on to the laptop. He thought he might get used to this VIP treatment in time. It wasn't really so bad.

'You picked a rough night to fly, Mr. Lindsey.' Zissler actually held the door open for him.

'Cletus Berry picked a rough night to get murdered.'

Zissler started the engine and put the sedan into gear.

Even at this hour of the morning, and even in miserable, freezing, wet December weather, the freeway leading into Manhattan was jammed.

2

Lindsey scrunched down inside the futon, alternately cursing himself for not calling ahead for a hotel reservation and either Mrs. Blomquist or Corporate Travel for not thinking to ask if he needed one. No, it was his own fault for relying on Morris Zissler's judgment.

It was *cold*. Of course — this was an office building; why would the landlord provide heat late at night? Fortunately, Berry had brought in a space heater. It helped a little.

In his travels with International Surety, Lindsey had always stayed in comfortable accommodations. But when Moe Zissler asked Lindsey where to drop him off, Lindsey had no answer. Zissler had suggested his using Cletus Berry's *pied-à-terre*, and after a moment's hesitation Lindsey had agreed. Zissler rattled a key to the place, and when he drove through the Queens Midtown

15

Tunnel and through Manhattan's slushy streets, Lindsey got his first real look at New York.

He'd have to learn the city fast if he was going to do anything with this puzzle. It was the first time he'd taken a case for International Surety where the company had no financial stake. Normally Desmond Richelieu would have squelched any effort like this one; but for all the Director's faults, he was loyal to his troops, and he wasn't going to let Cletus Berry's murder stand as just one more statistic in the most murderous country in the world.

Zissler drove uptown for a few blocks, then stopped in front of a nondescript commercial building on West 58th Street. 'This is it.' He got out and opened the door for Lindsey.

Torrington Tower. That was the name of the building, engraved into the granite lintel above the thick glass and tarnished cast-iron doors. Lindsey craned his neck. The Torrington Tower might have been considered a tower when it was erected, but now it was dwarfed by its neighbors.

16

Zissler separated a pair of keys from a massive batch. 'I had an extra set made when I heard you were coming to town, Mr. Lindsey. There's a guard in the lobby, but we've got keys to both the lobby door and to Mr. Berry's office.'

He hauled Lindsey's flight bag out of the sedan's trunk. Lindsey clung to his laptop computer in its carrying case. Zissler opened the lobby door and stood aside while Lindsey entered. The door locked itself behind them with a click.

The guard was behind his desk and stood up when Zissler and Lindsey entered. He'd been reading; now he laid his book down on his desk, spine upward. Lindsey read the title: *Principles of Modern Accounting for the Medium-Sized Business*.

The guard was a tall Hispanic with rich wavy hair and a small mustache. He wore a nametag that said *R. Bermudez*. 'Hello, Mr. Zissler,' he said. 'This gentleman with you?'

'This is Mr. Lindsey. Lindsey, Rodrigo Bermudez.'

The guard smiled and shook Lindsey's

hand. 'Please just call me Rigo.'

Zissler led the way to a small elevator that creaked its way up six stories. On the way up, Zissler said, 'Rodrigo's twin brother works here, too. Can't tell 'em apart except by their schoolbooks. Rodrigo's studying accounting. Benjamino's out to be a lawyer.'

Once they reached Cletus Berry's erstwhile home away from home, Zissler put down Lindsey's flight bag, then handed him the keys. 'Didn't the coroner or police put a seal on this place?' Lindsey asked.

Zissler shook his head. 'This is New York, Mr. Lindsey.'

Lindsey reached for his pocket organizer. He opened it and said to Zissler, 'I want to make sure I've got this right. The detective on the case is named Marcie Sokolov. You've met her?'

'No, just spoke with her on the telephone.'

Lindsey tightened his lips. This guy wasn't going to be much help. He wanted desperately to please, but unless you kept the instructions simple, he was more likely to mess up than to help out.

'What was your impression of this, ah, Detective Sokolov?'

'She was okay.'

Lindsey looked around the office for a chair. There was a nondescript gray rug on the floor and a couple of cheap prints of Rome on the walls. In addition to the computer, the microwave, and the futon, there were a desk with a telephone on it, a couple of chairs, and a filing cabinet. One window offered a view of Central Park. Lindsey recognized it from myriad movies and postcards. There were two other doors in the room. A bathroom complete with shower stall. Okay. And a closet. A rack of clothes, a dresserette. A shelf with a few pairs of shoes and a little TV set. The TV was one of those compact models with a built-in VCR.

Lindsey dropped to his hands and knees and scoped out the electrical connections under the desk. There was a power line for the computer, a fax/modem connection, and a TV cable outlet.

'She, um, Detective Sokolov asked me some questions,' Zissler added to his statement.

Lindsey stood up. 'What questions?'

'Well, like, Did Mr. Berry have any enemies? Use drugs? Did he go to Atlantic City often? Bet with bookies? Was he in debt? Did he run around with women?'

'And what did you tell her?'

'I told her no.'

'But you told me you hardly knew Berry. How did you know he didn't do any of that?'

'Well, that's right, I guess. But he didn't seem to have any enemies. Or the rest of it.'

'Women?'

'I never saw Mr. Berry with any women. I wouldn't know anything about that.'

Lindsey knew that Berry was married and had a daughter. Berry had mentioned his wife once or twice, but Lindsey couldn't remember him saying anything about a child. He had learned about the daughter from Berry's personnel file.

Cletus Berry had been a top worker; Lindsey could testify to that. He had a pleasant personality, he made good dinner-table conversation, and he had been an easygoing, unobtrusive room-mate. But he seldom spoke about his private life. Lindsey should have known that was a danger sign, but somehow he'd failed to pick up on it with Berry. *Put the dunce cap on me*, Lindsey thought. *There's more here than meets the eye.* 'Did Sokolov say what the police were planning to do about the killings?' he asked Zissler.

'About Mr. Berry and that other fellow? Well, Detective Sokolov said they were going to investigate fully.'

Lindsey sighed and looked at his watch. He'd readjusted it eastern time even though his body still thought it was two hours earlier.

Zissler said, 'I'd like to help out, Mr. Lindsey, but it's awfully late. I have to drive back out to Queens. My wife worries when I'm late.'

'Sure. I'll call you at Manhattan East if I need you.' As Zissler headed for the elevator, Lindsey could hear him humming.

Now Lindsey scrunched down inside the futon Berry had used. Why had Berry kept this place? He was entitled to office space at Manhattan East, but as a SPUDS agent he was authorized to set up a separate facility if he chose. It wasn't strange that Berry had preferred the privacy and independence of a separate office — but why a bed and a microwave oven? Why a TV? Why a closet full of clothing? Had Berry been leading a double life?

Lindsey had unpacked his flight bag and hung his suits in the closet along with Berry's. If there were any clues in the office, Lindsey would have to find them. If the police hadn't bothered to seal it off, there was no way they were going to send a forensics squad in to look for evidence.

What was Cletus Berry doing on Eleventh Avenue in the middle of the night, in the company of a petty mobster? It didn't make sense.

★ ★ ★

22

Lindsey awoke to cold, gray sunlight. He climbed out of the futon and pulled on a sweater and a pair of pants, then looked outside. The thoroughfares were filled with traffic. The accumulated sleet had already been shoved to the sides of the street, making shin-high gray-black berms along the curbs.

He looked at his watch: seven o'clock. He'd had less than three hours of sleep. He cleaned up, using Cletus Berry's little shower stall. Berry had left behind a plastic bottle of shampoo, and a razor on the sink. The only thing Lindsey had to provide for himself was a toothbrush.

He dressed in a gray woolen suit and overcoat and left the office, then rode down in the elevator. He passed a couple of business-people in the lobby and nodded. They ignored him.

A different guard sat at the desk in the front lobby. He looked up at Lindsey and frowned, clearly disturbed to see a stranger coming out of the elevator and leaving the building so early in the morning. Lindsey told the guard his name, and that he worked for International Surety and would be using the rented office for an indefinite time.

The guard looked more puzzled than ever. Like Rigo Bermudez, he wore a gray uniform with a Sam Browne belt; there was even a holster bucked to it. The guard was easily thirty years Bermudez's senior, and his uniform sleeve showed blue sergeant's chevrons. The plastic nametag attached to his uniform jacket said *Halter*. He wore half-glasses on the end of his nose and he'd been reading the *Daily News*. He had a bushy white mustache and white hair that stuck out from under his uniform cap.

The guard frowned. 'Linsley, is it?'

'Lindsey.'

'I know. That's what Mike Quill called the mayor. Linsley. Name was Lindsey. Did it just to irk him. Great man, he was.'

'Mayor Lindsay? I've heard of him. I don't think we're related.'

'Not Linsley. Mike Quill was the great man. Ran the transit union. Great man.' He laid down the newspaper and said,

'International Surety, hey? Some insurance outfit?'

'Right. Cletus Berry worked for us.'

'Oh, sure.' Daylight broke across the old man's face. 'Nice man. Pity, what happened. Pity.'

'How did you find out about it? Has anybody been here investigating?'

The guard laid his *Daily News* flat on his desk and turned it so Lindsey could see the front page. A huge headline announced, *BLOOD AND ICE!* Beneath it, in smaller type, *Santa Rubs Out Duo in West Side Alley.*

A stark black-and-white photograph filled most of the lower half of the page. It showed two bodies lying on an icy sidewalk, and a couple of corrugated metal garbage cans with some cardboard boxes behind them. The face of one corpse was thin, middle-aged, unshaven. The man wore what looked like a badly frayed, too-thin coat, and the splotches on it had to be blood.

The second corpse was better dressed, but the angle of the photo showed little of its face. That shortcoming was offset by a smaller photo, framed in an oval and inset in what would have been the right-hand third of the larger photo. It was the face of a black man wearing a white shirt and a dark necktie. You could see the edge of his suit inside his overcoat. His eyes were open and staring; they had the filmed-over look of the grisly post-mortem photos taken to celebrate nineteenth-century hangings. There was a perfect black dot above and between the eyes. On a Hindu, it might have been a caste mark. But on Cletus Berry's dark African American face, Lindsey knew that the dot was a bullet hole.

The guard said, 'You come to pay off on a policy?'

'No,' Lindsey replied, 'I'm here to find out who killed Cletus Berry.'

The guard opened his newspaper again. 'So, you going to be using Mr. Berry's office now?'

Lindsey nodded. 'For a while.'

'I hope you can do some good. Cops sure won't. Too busy with politics and graft. Same as ever.'

Lindsey reached for his wallet. He had

a discretionary fund, and this looked like a good time to be discreet. He extracted a couple of medium-large bills from his wallet. 'Mr. Halter — '

'Just call me Lou.' The bills disappeared. David Copperfield would have been proud. 'Anything I can do to help.'

'Isn't it a little bit unusual for a tenant to have his office furnished the way Cletus Berry's was? It looks as if he might have lived there sometimes.'

'I've never been in there. I wouldn't know.'

'But is it even legal?' Lindsey persisted.

Halter frowned. 'Building's zoned commercial, not residential. But I guess anybody can put a couch in his office, don't you think? And maybe a little kitchenette, and nuke a cup of soup if he feels like it. And if he's working late and he decides he wants to catch forty winks . . . I don't think it's nobody's business. Nobody's. Do you?'

'No.'

The lobby behind Lindsey was getting busy. People were arriving and the elevator was humming.

'I was wondering, Sergeant — ah, Lou.'

Halter looked at Lindsey over the tops of his glasses.

'What goes on in this building? It isn't exactly, well, the latest in posh surroundings, is it?'

Halter grinned crookedly. 'It'll probably get pulled down one of these days. But for now it's a great address, and it don't cost no arm and a leg to rent a little office. So you got a lot of little guys trying to look big in this building. Couple of music publishers and theatrical agents, half a dozen loan companies and lawyers. Shylocks and Sherlocks, I call 'em. Got a few outfits call themselves consultants, I wouldn't know for what.'

Lindsey grunted his thanks. It seemed unlikely that the killer was a fellow Torrington Towers renter, but you could never tell. Somebody who had it in for Berry might want to do his dirty work away from the building to keep the spotlight off himself.

Lou Halter had gone back to his newspaper. Lindsey crossed the lobby. In seconds he was part of the crowd passing on the sidewalk. Yep, it was Christmas. Christmas, and NFL playoff time.

Lindsey walked along 58th Street, looking for place to eat. The morning was still gray, but the sun was starting to fight its way through the clouds. He wasn't used to crowded sidewalks. Well, he'd adjust. He'd managed to speed up for Chicago and to slow down for New Orleans; he'd find the right pace for New York.

3

Lindsey wanted to talk with Berry's wife. He knew she'd be in shock. It was only 36 hours since the discovery of her husband's body, give or take a few hours, and she wouldn't even have begun to come to terms with his death. But sometimes that was a help. She wouldn't have edited her husband's life and death; she wouldn't have erected any barriers or sealed off any facts or memories that might have a bearing on the case.

Lindsey found a working payphone and looked up Cletus Berry's home number in his pocket organizer. It was a good thing he had the number with him. He dialed and a woman answered. She was crying. Lindsey identified himself, told the woman he was a friend as well as a colleague of Berry's, and asked if he could come and see her. She agreed, but not so early in the day, please; could he come in the afternoon? She spoke with a light Italian accent.

From Berry's personnel file, Lindsey had learned that Berry's wife was the former Ester Lazarini, an Italian citizen. Berry had married her in 1979, when he was serving as a warrant officer in the US Army, attached to a satellite NATO headquarters in Rome doing liaison work with the Italian Ministry of Defense. He made his appointment with her and hung up, then checked his wristwatch: a little after nine. He looked up another contact in his pocket organizer, punched Detective Sokolov's number, and introduced himself.

Marcie Sokolov had a pleasant voice but spoke with the hard-driving intensity that Lindsey thought typical of New Yorkers. 'You're with International Surety, interested in the Berry shooting? I already talked to your — ' She checked papers on her desk. ' — Morris Zissler. Have you spoken with him?'

Lindsey confirmed that Zissler had briefed him on the case, but that he was representing the company now in the matter of Berry's death. 'If you could spare a few minutes of your time?' he said. 'I flew in from Denver, and if I go back empty-handed . . . ' He let it hang there.

Sokolov took the bait. 'Okay. I'm at Midtown North. Where are you coming from? You know your way around New York? You taking a cab or the subway?'

'Uh — I'm on 58th Street, near Seventh Avenue.'

She laughed. 'Never mind. Welcome to our lovely city. You can walk here. Midtown North is on West 54th between Eighth and Ninth. Enjoy your stroll.'

Lindsey walked to the corner and stopped to buy a copy of *The New York Times*. He tucked it under his arm and started down Seventh Avenue.

Detective Sokolov might have meant to be ironic, but Lindsey really did enjoy it. He'd never seen such varied people jammed onto a single strip of pavement.

He reached Midtown North in a matter of minutes. The police were housed in an utterly characterless building that Lindsey quickly labeled as Postwar Functional. He gave his name to a bored civilian receptionist and sat down with his *New York Times* while he waited for Detective Sokolov.

The local stories were enticingly different. The most intriguing was a piece on the expected announcement of a race for the US Senate by a congressman named Randolph Amoroso. The resignation of the incumbent senator in the face of charges of sexual malfeasance and financial hanky-panky had left a vacant seat, and would-be senators were scurrying to qualify for a special election slated for June. Lindsey had barely heard of Amoroso, but apparently he was hot news in New York. A big Amoroso rally was planned for noon in Times Square. Lindsey looked at his watch. If he didn't spend too long in Sokolov's office, he might take a look at the event. He wasn't sure where Times Square was, but he suspected that it was fairly nearby.

Amoroso's congressional district was Dutchess County, wherever that was, but he was expected in New York to accept the endorsement of a right-wing radio personality. The event would be broadcast live on national radio and TV. Lindsey tracked back through the story to make sure that he'd got it right. He had. Amoroso was not yet an announced senatorial candidate, but he was issuing campaign manifestos and lining up endorsements anyway.

Reading the article about Amoroso, Lindsey felt a chill. An opponent was quoted as accusing the congressman of fascist leanings, and Amoroso's comment was only, 'I think I could make the trains run on time.' The Sons of Italy had disowned Amoroso, but a splinter group that claimed affiliation with a neo-fascist party in Italy had proclaimed its enthusiastic support, and Amoroso had welcomed it.

'These are true Americans,' the *Times* quoted him, 'and true Italian-Americans. These are the people who built our great land. In this age when welfare loafers, drug peddlers and deviants of every sort are wrecking our cities and our nation, it is time for real Americans to stand up and speak loud and clear — to city hall, to Congress and the Senate, and to the

White House itself.'

Lindsey frowned. The article went on like that, with periodical references to the greatness that once was Rome. A potential rival accused Amoroso of wanting to impose an Imperial *Pax Americana* on the world and on the country. Congressman Amoroso's rival was the mayor of the upstate community of Newburgh Heights. The rival's name was Oliver Shea. If Lindsey had barely heard of Amoroso before coming to New York, he was positive he'd never heard of Oliver Shea. Amoroso responded to Shea's charge by stating that a return to the age of the *Pax Romana* would mean the salvation of American civilization.

Lindsey laid the newspaper back on the bench as he watched a couple of uniformed cops drag a pair of young women past. Then he opened the paper again and leafed through it, searching for coverage of the dual murder of Cletus Berry and Frankie Fulton. He found the killings mentioned in a roundup piece on crime in the city. The article quoted Marcie Sokolov to the effect that the death of Frankie Fulton was one just more gang-related execution. Sokolov didn't say as much, but Lindsey got the feeling that she was perfectly happy to see mobsters removing one another from circulation. Berry's death was more puzzling, but Sokolov implied that even a solid citizen such as Cletus Berry seemed to be could get mixed up with the wrong type and find himself in big trouble.

The civilian receptionist caught Lindsey's attention with a shrill whistle and a sharp, 'Hey, you!' Lindsey dropped his newspaper. 'Upstairs, third floor, just ask for Sokolov. Here, don't forget to wear this visitor's badge.' Lindsey folded his *Times* neatly and left it on the bench.

Detective Sokolov's office wasn't an office at all, but a desk in a noisy bullpen. Marcie Sokolov was a petite woman with glossy black hair, an olive complexion, and sharp features. She was wearing a pale blue blouse and a patterned pullover sweater. Her detective's badge was pinned to her sweater.

Sokolov put down a coffee cup and stood up when Lindsey approached her desk, extending her hand. 'I suppose you have ID?'

He nodded and showed Sokolov his driver's license and IS credentials.

'You related to the mayor?'

'No.' He shook his head.

'What's wrong with Zissler? How come they sent you out here from Denver?'

Lindsey stood uncomfortably.

'Anyway, take a load off.' Sokolov pointed to a hard chair.

Lindsey cleared his throat. 'Mr. Zissler comes from our Manhattan East office. He has his other duties. I'm from SPUDS — Special Projects Unit/Detached Status. Cletus Berry was part of SPUDS. He was my friend. I wanted to do what I could do.'

Sokolov looked up at Lindsey with big dark eyes beneath jet-black eyebrows. 'When a man's partner is killed he's supposed to do something about it,' she said.

Lindsey said, 'That's right.' He recognized the line but didn't say anything else.

'However, this is a matter for law enforcement, Mr. Lindsey. We have something like 16,000 police officers in New York. Hundreds of detectives. Evidence technicians. Laboratory analysts. The DA's office. Prosecutors and courts and jails. This city spends a fortune on law enforcement.' She frowned. 'What makes you think you can do anything we can't do?'

'When a man's partner is killed,' Lindsey repeated Sokolov's line. 'Doesn't Bogie say that?'

'*Maltese Falcon* by Dashiell Hammett. Sam Spade speaking to Brigid O'Shaughnessy.'

'The line is in the movie, too.'

'I know that. And it's true. My partner is out on a bust. If anything happened . . . ' She paused. ' . . . I'd do something about it, you can bet on that. But then it'd be bye-bye Roscoe, and I'd have to get myself another partner. Life is hard, cowboy.' She picked up a folder and laid it down again. 'Okay, what do you need to know? What can you give me that I don't have already?'

Lindsey heard a slight scuffle and looked up. A young man in an immaculate three-piece suit and what looked like a hundred-dollar haircut was approaching with a scruffy-looking older man in a torn sweatshirt and faded jeans. The scruffy man had a badge pinned to his sweatshirt. The younger man was handcuffed.

As they passed Detective Sokolov's desk, Sokolov grinned at them. The scruffy man said, 'Yowza, mama.'

'Cat's pajamas,' Sokolov replied. 'Congratulations, Roscoe.' To Lindsey she said, 'Speak of the devil.'

Lindsey said, 'Moe Zissler put me up at Cletus Berry's office on 58th Street. His little place. There's a futon there, and a microwave.'

'Yeah. In the old days it would have been an army cot and a hotplate. What else is different?' Sokolov said.

'Well, don't you think there might be evidence there? I mean, the man is killed. You're supposed to be detectives down here. There wasn't even crime scene tape on the place.'

'It wasn't a crime scene, now, was it?' Sokolov spread her hands as if she couldn't understand Lindsey's need to have this explained. 'Berry was killed in

Hell's Kitchen. Look, Mr. Colorado, I'll make a deal with you. I won't sell life insurance, and you don't try and solve homicides.'

'You don't get it,' Lindsey said. 'Somebody murdered Cletus Berry and — '

'For the last time, what do you think he was doing in an alleyway with Frankie Fulton? Sneaking a little kiss?'

Lindsey shrugged.

'I don't know either,' Sokolov furnished. 'But you can bet it was nothing he'd want to tell his scoutmaster about. People who are clean don't get mixed up with the likes of Frankie Fulton. I'd like to know what it was all about, and I expect to find out. All in good time.'

'Then how come you didn't seal off Berry's little pad?'

Sokolov grinned. 'We were in there by noon yesterday. I was there myself. We turned up nothing. *Nada. Nicht.*'

'Oh.'

'That's why there was no tape. We rifled through his filing cabinet. Nothing. We peeked into his computer. Looked like routine insurance matters to me. In fact, you might want to take a gander yourself and see if there's anything strikes you funny. Give me a call if there is.' She stood up.

'Wait a minute,' Lindsey stopped her. 'Did you have a search warrant? How did you get in there?'

Sokolov looked annoyed. 'We didn't have a warrant and we didn't need a warrant. Your Mr. Zissler kindly informed us that your company pays the rent on Berry's little nest. Zissler has a key and he let us in. Is that okay with you?'

Lindsey felt the anger he'd been building for Sokolov drain from him. Reluctantly, he nodded.

'Now if you don't mind,' Sokolov said, 'I have to go powder my nose.' When she stood up, Lindsey saw that she was wearing fresh new jeans to go with her blouse and sweater. She had a holster strapped to her belt and the grip of what looked like a revolver sticking out of it.

It was still too early to visit Cletus Berry's widow. Lindsey stood outside Midtown North watching the traffic, then asked a stranger for directions and learned how to get to Times Square. It wasn't far. He started walking. Band music was playing through a loudspeaker, and he could hear voices, but he couldn't make out what they were saying.

When he got closer he found himself on the edge of a mob. Brawny individuals in neat suits were striding around, eyeing people who approached. There was something about them that made him uncomfortable. They were wearing lapel pins, and Lindsey passed a vendor selling buttons that seemed to have the same design. Each button was attached to a campaign pamphlet. It looked like a Roman chariot pulled by a team of horses. He bought one, and slipped the button and pamphlet into his overcoat pocket.

It must have taken amazing political clout to have Times Square shut down, even for a few minutes. Amazing clout to shut it down any time; but this was the middle of the day, on a business day, counting down to Christmas.

Lindsey moved into the mass of people. He didn't see any opening in the crowd, but somehow a limousine managed to move down Broadway, rolling through a narrow lane, and a number of people climbed out. One was the broadcaster who'd been mentioned in the morning newspaper. Lindsey recognized another, Congressman Randolph Amoroso, from his photo in the *Times*. A well-dressed woman was affectionately holding on to Amoroso's arm: the perfect political wife. Fourth was a distinguished middle-aged fellow with silvery temples and silver-rimmed glasses, a dark blue suit and a wine-red tie.

TV lights glared. Some functionaries ushered the party to a microphone on the steps of a monument. Behind the microphone, the doughboys who fought in the Great War were memorialized forever. They had caught three-quarters of a century of pigeon droppings for their trouble. A couple of other flunkies were setting up a covered display behind the congressman.

The radio personality took the microphone, gestured for the music to be cut off, and started warming up the crowd with a series of jabs at the president, the president's political party, and Mr. Oliver Shea. Finally he introduced Congressman Randolph Amoroso from the great city of Poughkeepsie in the great county of Dutchess.

Amoroso stepped to the microphone. The sun shone through and brightened Amoroso like a spotlight. It reflected off his bulbous, bald skull like a halo. It glinted off a silvery pin in the congressman's lapel. 'Just an hour ago,' Amoroso said, 'on the steps of my home in the beautiful Hudson Valley, I formally announced a great crusade for the heart and soul of America. I announced my candidacy for the Senate of the United States. I've been informed that I will be opposed in my bid by a very decent and intelligent man . . . ' He grinned as the crowd rustled. There were a few boos. ' . . . and a well-intentioned man.' Some shrill whistles. 'But my opponent is thoroughly out of touch with the times. He offers us the same old solutions that were tried and failed ten, twenty, thirty years ago . . . ' Amoroso paused. More shrill whistles. '*I* say that anybody who sells dope to a kid should be shot.' There were cheers. 'Anybody who sells porn to a kid — or who sells kiddie porn to anybody — should be shot.' More cheers. 'And anybody who tries to foist a filthy, degraded lifestyle on a decent, God-fearing America — '

His audience responded in unison: '*Should be shot!*'

Amoroso's voice boomed through the loudspeakers. 'Right you are, my friends. Right you are.' He waited for another round of applause and cheers. Then: 'My well-intentioned opponent — and his tweed-jacketed cronies at the universities and on the talking-head shows — accuse me of wanting to make America into a new Roman Empire.' He tilted his head and grinned. The sunlight actually sparkled off his oversized teeth. 'Well, an honest citizen could walk down the main street of Julius Caesar's Rome and not get mugged, my friends. Nobody tried to sell him a syringe full of poisonous dope. And nobody offered to sell him a magazine full of kiddie porn, either.' He shook his head ruefully. 'The new Roman Empire?' He paused for a beat. 'I think it's a *great* idea.'

Behind him, a tarpaulin was pulled from a giant poster. The poster showed a Roman chariot pulled by a team of rearing horses. The congressman beamed as his wife gazed at him adoringly. The broadcast personality clapped him on the shoulder, grabbed the microphone, and started working the audience again. The television lights in front of the doughboy monument winked off, one by one. Randolph Amoroso, Mrs. Amoroso, and the rest of his entourage climbed into their limousine, made a U-turn, and sped away, going the wrong way up closed-off, one-way Broadway.

The crowd dispersed. Lindsey checked the time, then headed for a subway entrance.

4

One thing about Cletus Berry — he hadn't talked about his private life, but he talked about New York. He wasn't a native — he'd revealed that much — but he'd taken to the city like a native, and over drinks at SPUDS conferences he'd told stories about New York with obvious pride in his voice.

His favorite was the story of the Second Avenue subway. The city had planned a whole new line to serve the East Side, got a referendum past the voters, and floated a multi-billion-dollar bond issue to pay for it. They'd torn down the elevated rail line that served that part of the city, the famous Third Avenue El. They even broke ground for the new subway line, but when it came time to start serious work they looked at their bank account and discovered that billions of dollars had somehow disappeared.

'One thing about New York politicians,' Berry had roared with laughter, 'they may be crooks, but at least they're not petty crooks.'

Cletus Berry had lived in an old red-brick one-time high-rise in the East 70s. The building might be a little past its prime; Lindsey formed the impression of solid, upper-middle-class urbanites. An awning over the sidewalk, a doorman in a modest dark blue uniform. A lobby with neutral-colored walls, a couple of gilt-framed mirrors, a flagstone floor. As Lindsey entered the lobby, a broad-shouldered middle-aged black man emerged from the elevator and crossed the lobby to the street door. Lindsey was startled; in that fleeting moment, the man bore an uncanny resemblance to the dead Cletus Berry. Lindsey blinked and the man was gone.

He entered an elevator operated by another blue-uniformed minion, a woman this time. She asked politely for Lindsey's floor, and whom was he planning to visit. He told her and she responded, 'Oh, it was such a pity. Mr. Berry was such a nice man; it was such a tragedy. Are you a friend of the family?'

'Mr. Berry was my partner.'

When Lindsey pushed the button beside the massive maroon-painted door, a small dog started to yip inside the apartment. Lindsey identified himself to the black-swathed woman who answered the door and she invited him inside.

The woman's gray hair was unkempt and her dress hung on her. This was no smart mourning outfit. This woman was no Auntie Mame. This was real grief. The woman offered her hand and Lindsey shook it, then dropped it. The woman's eyes were a dark green and her skin was olive. Her features were soft. She was a classic Mediterranean type.

He asked, 'Are you Mrs. Berry?'

She shook her head. 'I am her sister.' She spoke with a heavier Italian accent than the woman who'd answered the phone earlier; that must have been Berry's wife. 'She just came home. She wanted them to give her his body. They won't give her his body. She's with the baby now. Come in the house and sit down, you want to talk to her.'

He followed her inside. The yapping had come from a tiny dog with a glossy black-and-gold coat. The dog was circling Lindsey and the woman, darting forward as if it intended to nip at Lindsey's pants cuffs, then dancing back, its fore-end close to the hardwood floor, its hindquarters and stumpy tail elevated.

The woman said, 'Ezio Pinza, shame, you don't be a bad boy. You go keep Anna Maria company.'

The dog looked up at her. He gave one more yip. The woman gestured at him, as if she were brushing him away. 'Go, you. She's crying, you go.' The dog ran down a narrow hallway and scratched on a wooden door. The door opened and the dog disappeared into another room.

'You come and sit down,' the woman said to Lindsey. She led the way into the living room. A blue-patterned sofa and two easy chairs were grouped around a low table. Lindsey followed instructions.

The woman said, 'I am Zaffira Fornari. I am going to be with my sister. You wait. She know you are coming here, so she sees you.' She walked along the hallway the little dog had scampered down and rapped softly on the door. If there was a reply, Lindsey didn't hear it. She opened the door and disappeared behind it. In a moment the door closed with a metallic click.

Lindsey looked around the room. A fireplace on one wall, two massive bookcases opposite. A large frame, obviously holding a picture or a mirror, but now there was no telling which because it was draped in heavy black cloth. A couple of windows overlooking the street.

The woman had introduced herself as Zaffira Fornari, the sister of Berry's widow. Lindsey knew that Berry's wife was Ester Lazarini Berry; then her sister must be Zaffira Lazarini Fornari. Whoever Fornari was — obviously a husband.

The bookcases were jammed, and Lindsey's curiosity was just getting the better of him, pushing him to get up and scan the titles, when the bedroom door opened. Ester Lazarini Berry emerged; her sister Zaffira remained behind.

Ester might have been beautiful once. She might have been beautiful yesterday, until she learned of her husband's death. Now her face was drawn, her eyes were red from weeping, and her shoulders were rounded. She looked as if she was drawing in upon herself, racing to immerse herself in her thoughts and her memories and away from the world in which the body of her husband had to be chopped off the icy concrete in a garbage-strewn alley.

The sisters bore a strong mutual resemblance. Lindsey stood up when Ester Lazarini Berry entered the room. Like Zaffira, she was dressed in black. She walked toward Lindsey, almost steady on her feet. He stood up and started to say something but she took his hand in hers, not the way one person shakes hands with another, but the way a child takes the hand of an adult.

She said, 'You were his friend.'

'Yes.'

'I do not understand. Why did they kill him? I went there today; I had to look at him. Who would do that? They killed that other man, too; I did not know him. Maybe he did something, maybe he needed to die. But Cletus needed to live. I need him. Anna Maria needs him.'

She hadn't let go of Lindsey's hand, so he held her hand in both of his. She had graceful fingers and fine bones. She was trembling gently, steadily.

'We need him,' she repeated. 'He has a baby. Ten years old. You know what it mean to a little girl, ten years old, they kill her father? Why did they have to kill him?'

Lindsey shook his head. 'I came because — '

She pulled her hand away and said, 'Sit. You like a cup of coffee?'

He stammered a reply.

'Sit.'

He sat on the couch and watched her disappear into what must be the kitchen. He heard china and silver clattering. From the other room he heard the soft sounds of voices and sobs.

The bedroom door opened and Ezio Pinza pranced out on the end of a leash. He gave a small yelp when he saw Lindsey. The girl holding his leash — she must be the ten-year-old, Anna Maria — looked at Lindsey, then looked away. Zaffira Fornari was close behind her.

Anna was wearing a bright red-and-green mackinaw. Ezio Pinza wore a blue doggie sweater. Zaffira had put on a dark, shapeless coat and tied a black woolen scarf over her graying hair. They went to the front door, Ezio tugging at Anna. Zaffira reached over the girl's shoulder to open the latch. Just before the door closed behind them, Zaffira Fornari looked back at Lindsey and said, 'We go for a walk. Anna Maria's dog got to go for his walk.'

Ester returned from the kitchen carrying a tray with a silver coffee service and cups. She poured a cup for Lindsey and pushed a silver creamer and a little silver cup of honey with a miniature ladle in it toward him.

'You came to offer condolences, Mr. Lindsey.' Ester's English was better than her sister's; the accent barely discernible, the syntax perfect. 'He told me about you, that he knew you from Denver. He told me about the case he helped you with, on Mosholu Parkway. He always thought the Bronx was an exotic land. Or another planet. He used to joke with me about going to Mars. That was the Bronx. He called New Jersey Alpha Centauri, another galaxy.'

She paused and asked if his coffee was all right. He took a sip and said it was excellent. Now she poured a cup for herself, and took a sip.

'No more Mars. No more Alpha Centauri. I told him a thousand times, Alpha Centauri isn't another galaxy. It's our closest neighboring star. I studied astronomy as a girl, did you know that?'

Lindsey shook his head.

'I studied astronomy and history. I was going to be an astronomer or an historian, I hadn't made up my mind. But there wasn't much chance for me to do either of those in Italy. Maybe a schoolteacher, and teach history to schoolchildren. But then along came my handsome American and swept me off my feet. It was a scandal, me marrying Cletus, can you understand that?'

Lindsey could. He knew what it was

like to be part of an interracial couple. He knew what it was like to be dumped, even though Marvia had said she still loved him. 'It's the race thing, isn't it?' he'd asked Marvia, and she'd admitted that yes, it was. And that had been that, and now she was married to a man she could walk down the street with, without drawing stares.

'I think I can understand,' Lindsey said.

'Pardon me, Mr. Lindsey, if I doubt that. I don't think you know who the Lazarinis are.'

'Cletus was my good friend,' Lindsey said. A little diplomatic exaggeration couldn't hurt. 'But he was a private man, wasn't he?'

Ester Berry said, 'He was a private man.' Her smile was as rueful as it was faint.

'So, ah, we talked about our work, mainly. We were roommates, you know.'

'Women?'

Lindsey blushed. 'Not really.'

'Do not be ashamed. We women talk about men. We do it all the time, all our lives. Little girls talk about their brothers and their fathers. Big girls talk about their boyfriends. Grown women talk about their husbands. Mothers talk about their sons.'

Lindsey didn't have an answer.

'Widows,' Ester said. She drank more coffee, then put her cup down carefully on its saucer. 'Widows. Now I will learn what widows say about men.' She started running her fingers along her cheekbones, then clasped them in her lap. 'My mother used to say that we were the first Jews in Rome. We were there before the Christians. We were there before Joshua ben Joseph was born. Do you know that, Mr. Lindsey? Do you believe me?'

Lindsey was startled. 'I don't really know. I didn't know you were, ah, Jewish, Mrs. Berry. I didn't even know there were Jewish people in Italy. I mean, it's such a Catholic country.'

'Are you Catholic, Mr. Lindsey?'

Lindsey shook his head. He didn't want to say that he was nothing. He'd been raised without religion, and with a careful, politically correct omission of ethnicity. 'No, I'm not Catholic.'

'You were never in a Jewish house of mourning? We don't sit shiva, not the way we should. But we cover the mirrors, the pictures. And how can we stay home? The dog has to go out; does he understand the Law? And the baby, she has to take the dog, and her aunt has to protect the baby. Even in this neighborhood.'

She sighed and brought herself back on track. 'They think that Italy is their country, the Christians. Even the ones who hate their church. But there were Hebrews in Rome in Caesar's day. Did you know that? There were free Hebrew traders, and there were Jewish slaves in Caesar's own household. There were Hebrew prayers at Caesar's funeral, did you know that? No, I didn't think so. The Lazarinis trace their blood to those times. My first ancestor came to Rome from Athens with trade goods and gifts. Do you believe that?'

Lindsey didn't know what to say. He remained silent.

'He settled in Rome and studied silversmithing. That became his trade. He was tired of traveling and he wanted to settle down. He found a nice Jewish girl and married her, and there have been Lazarinis in Rome for 2,000 years. More.'

Lindsey heard the sound of a key in the heavy front door of the apartment, and the sounds of Zaffira and Anna Maria with the little dog returning from their walk. He swiveled on the couch to watch. They had a few snowflakes on them, and the woman brushed the girl, then the girl brushed the dog, before they came down the hall. Behind him, Lindsey could hear Ester's voice continuing.

'There were Jews in the Roman Senate, did you know that? Two thousand years ago. And there were Jewish soldiers, officers, generals, yes, in King Umberto's army in the First World War. Commanders. Medal winners. They were Lazarinis.'

The older woman and the girl came into the living room. They had left their coats in the front hallway. Even the dog had left his sweater in the hallway, and stood in his short, glossy black-and-gold coat, hiding behind Anna's feet, peering around her at Lindsey.

Ester put her arms around the young girl and said, 'Mr. Lindsey, this is my daughter, Anna Maria Berry. Cletus is her father.'

She hadn't got used to referring to her husband in past tense. That wasn't surprising, since the police hadn't released his body to the widow for burial.

'Anna, Mr. Lindsey was your father's friend. He's come to help us.'

Lindsey studied the girl's face. Her skin was darker than her mother's, but Ester's Mediterranean olive and Cletus Berry's African American black had blended well. Her hair was glossy black and thick. She wore it in pigtails, not yet switching to teenage sophistication. She was slim, almost wispy. She wore a plaid shirt, new-looking jeans, and tennis shoes. He felt a sudden pang, then realized its source. Anna's skin was hardly lighter than Jamie Wilkerson's, Marvia Plum's son by her first husband. He had almost been Lindsey's stepson. He was the same age, and if things had gone differently in California, Jamie and Marvia might have been in New York now, and Jamie and Anna Maria might have become friends.

Lindsey blinked himself out of his reverie. Why had Cletus never mentioned his daughter? *If she were mine*, Lindsey thought, *she'd be the apple of my eye.* But the more he thought of Berry's friendly manner, his amusing conversation, his little history lessons and anecdotes, the more he realized that he'd learned nothing about Berry's personal life from their time together.

What do you say to a child whose father has just been murdered? 'It's a pleasure to meet you, Anna Maria.'

The girl had extended her hand halfway to Lindsey. Her dog had crept around her ankles and watched him suspiciously. He shook the girl's hand. To her mother, the girl said, 'Can I go to my room? I want to talk to Mosé.'

Ester shook her head. 'He doesn't know yet, Anna darling. I should call Abramo and Sara.'

Zaffira, standing behind Lindsey, said, 'I'll do it, sister. It's too much; you don't have to do that.'

'I already told him,' Anna said.

'You what?' Ester sat bolt upright.

'Last night. I couldn't sleep. I just sat in bed with Ezio and tried to read a book, but I couldn't, so I logged on and talked to Mosé. I know he told his parents. They'll probably phone you today.'

Ester nodded. 'All right, Anna. Go ahead.' Then, before the child could leave, Ester stopped her. 'You haven't said a word to Mr. Lindsey, Anna.'

The girl looked angrily at Lindsey. 'Mother says you're going to help us. How are you going to help us? My father is dead!' She burst into tears, then turned her back on Lindsey. Her shoulders shook.

Lindsey held his hand out before Ester could apologize. 'I *will* help you. I met Detective Sokolov.'

'So did I. She came here yesterday and talked to us. She isn't doing anything and I don't think you can do anything either.' She whirled, snatched up her dog, and ran to her room.

Zaffira had followed Anna to her room. Before long she returned and took the second easy chair facing Lindsey, along-side her sister.

'What did you think?' Lindsey asked.

Ester was calmer than she had been. 'I think Detective Sokolov was trying to be kind to us, to Anna Maria and me. I think she thinks Cletus was some kind of scumbag, and that was why he was with a scumbag when they were both shot. Excuse my language.'

'Which means that the NYPD isn't going to devote too much effort to trying to solve this crime. They're busier frying other fish.'

'Protecting Randolph Amoroso and his gang of fascists,' Zaffira put in. 'He makes me ashamed I am Italian.'

'I think Sokolov is doing her best, but I think she has the wrong idea. I don't think Cletus Berry was that kind of man, and I don't think he deserved to die like that kind of man. I'm here to find out what really happened.'

But he wasn't sure he was right.

5

Lindsey didn't know if Berry's deal with the building included trash service; if not, he'd dispose of the remains of his frozen meal himself. He'd overestimated his appetite and underestimated his fatigue. He sat in Berry's swivel chair and watched a few soft flakes falling outside the office window. He wasn't sure that staying here was such a good idea, but it would do for the time being.

Had he learned anything useful from his visit to Ester Lazarini Berry? A lecture on the history of the Jews of Rome. And Berry's wife was Jewish. But did her background have anything to do with her husband's murder? He didn't know, and he'd learned precious little else from his interview.

After Zaffira and Anna had returned from walking the little dog, Lindsey had thought it was time to leave; he'd intruded on their grief long enough. The household was in a state of disarray. The family needed to renew their mutual bonds. Friends and family might help, but the presence of an outsider would only add to their stress. So he'd left, stopped at a grocery store and bought a few supplies, and taken a cab back to West 58th Street.

Lindsey had put his few groceries away, then set up Berry's TV and turned on the local news while he used the microwave. There was controversy over Randolph Amoroso's rally in Times Square. The congressman's opponent in the race for the senate, Oliver Shea, got screen time to accuse the mayor of the city of New York of playing politics with the taxpayers' money.

'How dare the mayor shut down Times Square to stage a partisan political rally?' Shea demanded. 'How many police officers were diverted from the vital job of fighting crime and protecting our good citizens, to act as ushers for this sleazy playlet? As the mayor of a city myself, I can tell you that it cost a pretty penny. I demand that hizzonner the mayor bill my opponent's campaign for the full amount!'

The camera cut from Shea to a spokesperson for the mayor. The mayor and his family, it turned out, were conveniently out of town, attending a concert of sacred music composed by the late Duke Ellington, in the National Cathedral in Washington, D.C. Following the concert they expected to fly to Puerto Rico for a brief holiday.

No, the spokesperson explained, there was nothing political about the mayor's absence. And if there was anything irregular about the Amoroso rally in Times Square, the spokesperson was certain that hizzonner the mayor would look into it as soon as he returned to his desk in the New Year, and hizzonner took this opportunity to wish all New Yorkers a healthy, happy, and prosperous holiday season and blah blah blah . . .

Lindsey jerked away as the microwave beeped. His dinner was ready, but he was too sleepy to do more than pick at it. Afterwards he washed up and climbed into Berry's futon. There were times when Lindsey had done some of his best thinking lying in bed at night, staring at the ceiling and reviewing the day's events. There were other times when he'd found comfort in the presence of Marvia Plum. But tonight Marvia was almost 3,000 miles away, and there was no comfort for Lindsey in that.

He awke to the watery December sunlight waking him again. He put on a pair of socks to keep his feet warm, made himself a cup of instant coffee in the nuker, and sat it down at at Berry's desk.

He shuffled to the closet and took the button and pamphlet that he'd bought at the Amoroso rally the day before from his overcoat pocket. Then he returned to the desk, swallowed a sip of coffee, and opened the pamphlet. The front page featured a photo of Congressman Amoroso in a vaguely imperial pose, the familiar horse-and-chariot logo ghosted in behind him. The headline read AMERICA NEEDS AMOROSO and the minimal body type touched on a series of hot buttons. Apparently Amoroso was a reformer. In fact, his solution to every problem seemed simple and emphatic. One word. *Reform*.

Tax Reform!
Budget Reform!
Welfare Reform!
Education Reform!
Immigration Reform!
Law Enforcement Reform!

The centerfold of the pamphlet consisted of a review of Amoroso's brilliant career and endorsement statements from leading citizens, all superimposed on that ghostly chariot image.

Lindsey picked up the shiny button. There it was again, in glossy silver ink on an imperial purple background, and the word AMOROSO in glaring yellow letters. He sighed. He was learning more about Randolph Amoroso than he really cared to know . . . and next to nothing about Cletus Berry. Even so, it was all information that *might* suddenly fall into place to clarify a previously puzzling picture.

The pamphlet's last page was topped

by the chariot image, not ghosted this time, and a couple of paragraphs about its history, connecting it with the great men of history including Julius Caesar and the greatness that was Rome.

Lindsey shoved the pamphlet and button into a coat pocket; he was ready to forget about the Amoroso rally for the moment. He phoned Marcie Sokolov at Midtown North. She made it clear that she was a very busy police officer and that she didn't have time to chat with every amateur sleuth and detective wannabe who happened to take an interest in a strictly routine murder.

After that rebuff, Lindsey dressed for the outdoors and rode down in the elevator. Traffic in the lobby was light. The uniformed Lou Halter sat at his desk, coffee cup and *Daily News* in front of him. He looked up and nodded to Lindsey.

'Lou, how many hours do you work?' Lindsey asked. 'Is there a guard here around the clock?'

'Regular eight-hour shift. Me and the Bermudez boys, Rodrigo and Benjamino.

We swing through weekends, double shifts, so we can get a day off. Boss brings in temps for days like Christmas and Easter. I'd take the extra shift myself, it's golden time, but he won't go for it.' He stifled a yawn. 'The work isn't really too hard, see. I'm on Social Security, got nothin' else to do, so this job give some nice pocket money for my kids and grandkids. I don't need it. Rigo an' Mino, now, they're a couple of go-getters. Came here studyin' hard, the two of 'em. They're going places, believe you me.'

Lindsey gestured at the tabloid and asked if there was anything new on the Berry case. Halter pointed to a headline about the murders. 'Not a peep about Mr. Berry. But they've got some stuff here on Frankie the Four-flusher.' He tapped a photo. 'See that? I guess he knew his way around a little.' He turned the paper so Lindsey could see the photo.

Lindsey recognized the file shot of Frankie Fulton from the corpse photo in the previous morning's *News*. It showed Fulton in better days, posing in a nightclub with a prosperous-looking older man and a scantily clad showgirl. The clothing and hairstyles looked ten or fifteen years out of date. The cut-line identified Fulton as a 'onetime mob enforcer and café society habitué' and the showgirl as Millicent Martin, 'photographed shortly before her still unsolved gangland-style slaying.' The older man was identified as 'prominent antique dealer Alcide Castellini.'

Lindsey blinked. The older man looked oddly familiar too. Who was he? He tried to visualize him in color instead of monochrome.

And then he had it. The man in the photo was a younger version of the last man he'd seen climb from Congressman Randolph Amoroso's limousine at the Times Square rally. He looked up from the newspaper. 'You mind if I clip this?' he asked.

The guard pulled open a drawer in his desk and came up with a pair of sewing scissors. He handed then to Lindsey, who snipped out the photo and the accompanying story and put them in his pocket. He'd scanned the story itself. It added

71

nothing to what he already knew. But the photo had added two fresh players to the drama: Millicent Martin — probably a stage name, and Alcide Castellini. Martin had been murdered 'gangland style.' And Castellini was an antiques dealer. What could they and Fulton have to do with Cletus Berry?

Lindsey found a working payphone in a kiosk and punched for directory assistance. Apparently the vandals who had attacked payphones for decades had finally lost interest and moved on to bigger prey, but there wasn't a telephone book to be found.

There was no listing for Alcide Castellini.

Lindsey walked to a drugstore with an indoor phonebooth. A clerk loaned him a classified directory. There were antique dealers galore, and the closest concentration seemed to be on 57th Street. He walked the few blocks, turned the corner at the old Carnegie Hall, and found a row of antique stores.

He picked one at random and walked in. The store was filled with ornate gilt

72

furniture and elaborately framed paintings of elegant French ladies. A woman in a gray woolen suit was serving a lady customer. The transaction was just concluding, and Lindsey waited until the customer tuned to leave the shop before stepping forward.

Her nametag said *Cele Johnston*. She smiled at Lindsey. 'What may I show you, sir?'

Lindsey handed her an International Surety business card.

She read it and looked puzzled. 'I didn't think we'd entered an insurance claim of any sort.'

'No, I'm just looking for some information. This involves a death claim. A death under difficult circumstances. I'm just trying to clear up some questions about the decedent. We know that he was acquainted with an antiques dealer, and I thought you might be acquainted with him.'

She raised an eyebrow.

'The antique dealer's name is Castellini.

'I know him.'

'If you could put me in touch? A telephone number or address? Does he have a shop?'

Cele Johnston had gray eyes and blonde hair that was starting to streak with gray. She narrowed her eyes as if trying to peer directly into his brain. 'Come with me.'

She led the way past satin-covered sofas and delicate, polished, scroll-like chairs. She opened a door and said, 'Joseph, don't let any of the stock wander out. If browsers come in, be nice. If you get a live customer, call me.'

6

Cele Johnston sat behind a mahogany desk. Lindsey sat opposite her in what Sam Spade would have called a client's chair. She called it a Chippendale.

'Mr. Lindsey, why are you looking for Castellini? Was he the beneficiary of a policy your company carried?'

Lindsey shook his head. 'Nothing like that.'

'Well?'

'Ms. Johnston, have you ever heard of Cletus Berry?'

'No.'

'He was one of our employees. He was murdered two nights ago. The police don't seem to be taking the case very seriously. Berry was found in an alley in Hell's Kitchen. He was shot, execution-style, and there was another body with his — a small-time gangster named Frankie Fulton.'

'Mr. Lindsey, I'm really very sympathetic, but your story just isn't interesting.

I'm sorry if Mr. Berry was killed, but in all honesty, this sounds to me like a classic case of wrong place, wrong time. What was your friend doing in that neighborhood, in that kind of company?'

Lindsey spread his hands. 'That's what I'm trying to find out.'

'But what does Mr. Castellini have to do with it?'

'The *Daily News* ran a file photo showing three people: Frankie Fulton, a showgirl named Millicent Martin, and Alcide Castellini. Fulton is the link to Cletus Berry. They were murdered together. Millicent Martin is dead. The paper says that she was also murdered. That leaves only Castellini. If I'm going to unravel Cletus Berry's death, it's going to have to be through Alcide Castellini.'

Cele Johnston opened a drawer and laid a business card on top of her desk. From an elegant brass-and-marble holder she lifted a pen and wrote something on the card, then she slipped the card back into the drawer and slid it shut.

'Before I give this to you, I'm going to tell you a couple of things. But before I do that, I have to ask you a few questions.' She looked at Lindsey, waiting for him to accept her plan. He nodded. 'People think that the antiques business is all society folk and the love of elegant objects.'

Lindsey grinned. 'I'm an insurance adjuster, Ms. Johnston.'

'Cele.'

'Bart,' he said.

'That's right.' She nodded. 'I imagine you do know better than that. But you see, antiques can't be manufactured. Or at least they *shouldn't* be. But there are plenty of counterfeiters around. Antiques may seem to be a very genteel, very hoity-toity business, Bart, but in fact it's a tough, competitive racket. There's a lot of competition for merchandise, and there is just so much merchandise to be had. Just so many Strads, just so many Chippendales. Sometimes people play rough. Sometimes they play dirty.'

'You're talking about Castellini.'

'Alcide Palmiro Castellini. I didn't tell you anything about him. In fact, I don't know you.'

She slid the drawer open once more and handed him the card. All that it had on it was a seven-digit number.

★ ★ ★

Lindsey walked back to Seventh Avenue and bought a subway token. It was about time to learn some more about the fabulous New York City subway system. He rode a BMT train to Times Square. It was the middle of the day, and the cars were only half-full. Many of the passengers were carrying Christmas packages.

Lindsey climbed back into the pallid sunlight and chilly air and walked across 42nd Street to the New York Public Library. Finding his way to the newspaper room, he picked up an index to *The New York Times*. He found a vacant chair at a long wooden table and opened the index. There were three listings for *Martin, Millicent*. He noted the dates and pages, then returned the index to a clerk and requested microfilm copies of the *Times* for the dates of Millicent Martin's three appointments with destiny.

The first article was a review of an off-off-Broadway experimental performance piece; the review of the play, bylined Victor Hopkins, was scathing. But Hopkins concluded: ' . . . A single ray of light shines in the person of Millicent Martin, a young actor/singer/dancer who displayed a well-trained voice, fluid movements, and a compelling stage presence that deserve far better than the beating she takes in her brief role as the much-victimized Countess Specula.'

The second item, without a byline, was dated six months later. Millicent Martin, age 26, had apparently been awakened in the middle of the night in her basement apartment on East 5th Street. Neighbors reported nothing unusual, but police responded to an anonymous telephone tip and found her bound hand and foot, duct tape over her mouth and nose. Unable to free herself and remove the tape, she had suffocated. There was no sign of robbery or sexual assault, and no evidence of forceful entry. Police theorized that the victim was acquainted with her killer, and might have submitted voluntarily to the restraints as part of a sexual 'game.'

The third item was dated a month later. Martin was mentioned in it in passing, included in a list of 'unsolved, unthinkable, unforgivable atrocities' enumerated in a speech by Congressman Randolph Amoroso.

Lindsey made prints of the three items, then rewound the microfilm and returned it to the desk. He folded the fresh copies of the newspaper clippings and slipped them into his pocket. Then he asked a librarian where he could find a reverse telephone directory, and looked up the number on the card that Cele Johnston had given him. The number was written in a precise, feminine hand, in dark green ink.

Of course, Lindsey could just drop a coin in the telephone and try the number on Cele Johnston's card. But what would he say to Castellini? What if Castellini simply refused to take his call? At that point, Lindsey would be up against a stone wall. Better to bide his time, try to learn more about the ominous antiques dealer, and make his move when he was in a stronger position than he was right now.

Just for the hell of it he tried a normal Manhattan directory and searched its pages for Victor Hopkins. There was no listing for him, but in itself that meant little. Hopkins might live in one of the other boroughs, or he might have an unlisted number like Alcide Castellini.

He telephoned *The New York Times* from a payphone in the library and struggled with a voicemail system. Finally a real live human being identified herself as 'Arts. Amy Baines here.'

Lindsey asked for Victor Hopkins. The woman said that Hopkins didn't work for the *Times*. He was a freelance who occasionally picked up an assignment when the paper needed an extra reviewer, especially for more esoteric events. When Lindsey asked, she said it was against policy to give out addresses or telephone numbers. Lindsey explained that he was working on a case that involved Millicent Martin, the showgirl.

Now the woman responded. 'Victor really thought Millie was hot stuff. He dated her a couple of times. I didn't think they were a serious item, but you should have seen him when she got snuffed. For a while there I didn't think he was going to navigate.'

Lindsey waited. This was where the game got tricky.

'You have some information about Martin?' Amy Baines said. 'The cops never got anywhere. You're no cop, that's a slam dunk.'

'No.' Lindsey felt his pulse kick up a couple of beats. He was getting somewhere. 'I'm just an insurance man. But I'm investigating my partner's murder.'

'And when a man's partner is killed he's supposed to do something about it.'

Thank you, young lady. Thank you, Humphrey Bogart, and thank you, Dashiell Hammett, wherever you are.

'That's exactly right,' Lindsey said.

After a pause, the woman said, 'Give me your number. I'll call Victor. If he wants to talk to you, he'll call you. That's the best I can do.'

'I'm at a payphone.'

'Give me that number and wait there. I can always reach Victor.'

Lindsey complied, and waited. At length the telephone rang. He paused to catch his breath before he lifted the receiver. The young male voice on the other end asked who was calling. Lindsey identified himself.

The voice said, 'This is Victor Hopkins. You want to talk to me?'

'About Millicent Martin.'

'Where are you?'

Lindsey told him.

'Walk over to Third Avenue and head downtown. I'll meet you in half an hour at the White Rose. It's a saloon and hofbrau.'

'How will I know you?'

'Never mind. You just describe yourself. And you'd better give me a piece of ID. I don't want to seem melodramatic, but I'm taking a chance even meeting you. Where are you from?'

'Uh — California originally, but I work in Denver now.'

'That's a long commute. Okay. Good

enough. What do you look like? What are you wearing?'

Lindsey told him.

'Okay. I'll try and get to the White Rose first. If I don't, you go ahead and order a drink. I'll find you. I'll say, 'I heard it's snowing in Boston today,' and you answer, 'It was sunny in Denver.' You got that?'

'Sounds like a spy movie!'

'You want to talk to me, Mr. Lindsey? White Rose, half an hour, remember the script.'

★   ★   ★

Lindsey walked down the library steps and headed east. There were Christmas decorations in most of the store windows, and he passed more shoppers carrying shopping bags full of colorfully wrapped packages. It was snowing steadily. A few pedestrians carried umbrellas to keep the snow off their heads, though most relied on hats or scarves or simply let the flakes land on their hair.

Lindsey ducked into a hat store and

bought a fedora. He thought wryly that if he pulled down the brim of the hat and turned up the collar of his coat, he'd look like a real spy.

He turned on Third Avenue as Hopkins had instructed him and looked for the White Rose. It didn't take long to find it. He pushed through the swinging doors. The steam and the odors hit him even before the sight of the crowded room. With a start, he realized that he hadn't eaten today. He pushed his way to the pitted wooden counter and ordered a corned beef sandwich and a cup of coffee. As he waited he looked around, wondering if there was any way he could spot Victor Hopkins before Hopkins spotted him.

'Here ya go.'

Lindsey turned back to the counter. The sandwich looked delicious and the coffee was perfect for a day like this. He picked up the sandwich and took a bite. In the mirror behind the counter he caught a look at himself and his neighbors. On one side of him an old man was reading a copy of the *New York*

Post. The headline had something to do with a threatened strike.

' . . . snowing in Boston today.'

Lindsey couldn't hear the beginning of the sentence over the rumble of conversation in the room, but he got the important part. He was seated on a wooden bar stool. He started to swivel but the voice said, 'Nope.'

Instead of turning, he peered into the mirror. He wasn't sure which person behind him had spoken, but he had a pretty good guess. 'It was sunny in Denver.'

The voice behind Lindsey said, 'Go ahead and eat your sandwich.'

Lindsey took another bite and washed it down with coffee. He dropped a bill on the counter and slid backwards off his stool. This time Victor Hopkins didn't stop him.

'Let's get out of here.'

Hopkins led the way out of the White Rose. He looked to be in his late twenties or early thirties. He was taller than Lindsey but he weighed easily twenty pounds less. He wore dark-rimmed glasses that framed startling blue eyes, a small blond beard and mustache, and a knitted skiing hat. On the sidewalk he halted and faced Lindsey.

'Tell me who you are and what you want.' He reminded Lindsey of himself as he'd been fifteen or twenty years ago, and he felt a rush of envy for the younger man.

Lindsey said, 'I'm trying to find out who killed Cletus Berry.'

'Never heard of him. Amy said you were investigating Millicent Martin's death.'

'I am.'

'Look, I'm taking a chance talking to you at all. You'd better talk turkey to me or I'm gone.'

'Berry was my friend. He was shot. They found him in an alley a few days ago.'

'Oh, okay. I didn't get his name. I saw the picture, though. I get it now. Your pal was that overdressed black dude who got killed with Frankie Fulton.'

'That's right.'

'You're not a cop.'

'Not at all.' Lindsey handed him an International Surety business card.

Hopkins turned the card over, then shoved it into his pocket. 'Of course, anybody could make one these with a laser printer nowadays.'

'What do I have to do? Get real, Mr. Hopkins. What would I be up to, if I'm not bona fide?'

Hopkins pursed his lips. 'Okay. Let's go find a place to sit.' He led Lindsey to a Christian Science reading room. They found two chairs in a corner and sat facing each other. Hopkins picked up a copy of *The Christian Science Monitor* mounted on a wooden rod and spread it across his lap. He leaned back and said, 'Fill me in.'

Lindsey told him the story, as much of it as he knew. When he finished, Hopkins said, 'All right. Frankly, I don't really care that much about your pal Berry. But I do care about Millie.'

'You and she were an item?'

Hopkins gave him a bitter grin. 'I guess you could say we were an item.'

'And when she was killed, the police

weren't interested, were they?'

'Not very.'

'Is that the way it is in New York? I mean, I've heard that New Yorkers don't even bother to report burglaries and the like, but — murder?'

'They pay attention to serious crimes if they think there's anything they can do. Or if the victim is rich or famous. Or if the crime is particularly gruesome. High-profile stuff. *Daily News* or *Post* screamer stuff. Evening news footage on Channel Two.'

'The *Daily News* described Millicent Martin as a showgirl. But your review of her in the *Times* made her seem like . . . ' Lindsey didn't know what the review had made her seem like.

Hopkins snorted. 'She was talented. She was a sweet little Italian girl from a town in Pennsylvania where everybody else was Polish. The Martinellis, with the Kystowskis on one side and the Wajowiczes on the other. You know the story, Lindsey.'

Lindsey said nothing.

'She went to Mass every Sunday. The

priest wanted her to become a nun; her parents wanted her to find a nice Italian boy and get married and make babies. She couldn't wait to get out of there and come to New York and get famous. She did all the standard stuff — class plays, homecoming queen. She got to New York and she went a little crazy.'

'How long did you know her?'

'Only a year. I saw her in that God-awful performance piece. You wouldn't believe what a pile of crap can get produced in this town.'

'But you said that she was good, in your *Times* review.'

'*She* was talented. A real Italian beauty. Blue-black hair, lovely skin. And I fall in love with this wonderful little Italian Catholic girl and she gets murdered.' He locked eyes with Lindsey. 'She was going to move into my place. She'd got into a real mess, but she cleaned up her act; she was doing okay. But they caught up with her and wouldn't let her go. So . . . ' He made a helpless gesture. 'I don't want to talk anymore.'

'But I need to talk to you,' Lindsey

pressed him. 'What was Millicent's connection to Fulton? To Castellini? We haven't scratched — '

'Maybe another time.'

'How can I reach you? I can't just call the *Times*.'

Hopkins stood up and started toward the street. Lindsey followed him. He said, 'Come on, Victor. You can't just leave me hanging.'

Hopkins stopped. 'All right. Give me your number. I'll call you when I'm ready to talk again. That's the most I can offer.'

Lindsey found another International Surety card and wrote the number of Berry's answering machine at the 58th Street apartment on it. Hopkins shoved it into his pocket and pushed his way onto Third Avenue, disappearing into the crowd of pedestrians.

7

Lindsey phoned Berry's East Side apartment and spoke with Zaffira Fornari. He told her he'd like to talk with Ester Berry once more.

Zaffira asked, 'Did you not get your answers before when you were here?'

'There are just a few more questions, if that wouldn't be too much trouble.' Straight out of a *Columbo* rerun, he thought wryly.

'We got the autopsy report today. My sister is very upset. It made her cry.' There was a pause, then Lindsey heard Zaffira sigh. 'Well, you come ahead. Maybe to talk will help her. You are coming now?' He confirmed he was coming now.

Lindsey was getting the hang of this town. He climbed aboard a Third Avenue bus, paid his fare and found a seat. On reaching for his pocket organizer, he discovered he still had the pamphlet and button that he'd got at yesterday's Amoroso for Senate rally. He turned the pages of the pamphlet idly. Who was the scholar they quoted about the fabled chariot? William Van Huysen, Ph.D., Yale University. *Huh. Nothing if not classy.*

He looked over his shoulder at the passing street scene. Moving uptown, Third Avenue was lined with posh shops and restaurants. He couldn't see the sky, but the afternoon was growing dark. The snow was continuing to fall.

Before he slipped the pamphlet back into his pocket, Lindsey read Professor Van Huysen's little essay again. It was only three paragraphs long.

The Silver Chariot of Caesar — actually a silver chariot drawn by a brace of horses sculpted of finest marble — has a long history. Its origins are shrouded in mystery. Legend has it that King David ordered it crafted as a plaything for his son Solomon. In later years it made its way to ancient Hellas, where Philip of Macedon taught the youthful Alexander to use it in planning his later conquests.

Carried to Rome by an itinerant Greek, it was presented to Julius Caesar when Caesar was but a child. The chariot brought him good fortune in war and in politics, but was lost to history shortly before Caesar's assassination. Some scholars believe that Charlemagne played with the toy chariot before becoming Holy Roman Emperor in the year 800.

For over a thousand years the chariot was reported in different parts of the world, only to disappear again and again. It was last exhibited in the Italian Pavilion at the New York World's Fair of 1939. In 1940 the chariot was supposed to be returned to Italy, but it never arrived there and has not been seen since.

Lindsey dropped the pamphlet back into his pocket. *Bogie*, he thought, *where are you now that we need you?*

The bus stopped at 72nd Street and Lindsey walked another block, turned right for half a block, and entered the Berrys' apartment building.

The elevator operator asked, 'Here for the Berrys again?' Lindsey nodded.

* * *

'Mr. Lindsey.' Ester Berry extended her hand and Lindsey shook it again. He'd been ushered to the couch once more. Today Zaffira Fornari served tea and joined them. Anna Maria, she explained, had taken Ezio to visit her friend Shoshana across the street. The sisters both wore black, as they had the previous day.

Lindsey left his organizer in his pocket. He opened a little notepad and turned the barrel of his gold International Surety pencil. 'Mrs. Berry,' he said, 'I know this must be hard, but if you wouldn't mind . . . '

Ester Berry sighed. 'You have to be better than that Sokolov woman. She called me this morning with the results of the autopsy. She said she was sending a copy later.' She squeezed her eyes shut and shook her head. 'You want to know what Detective Sokolov told me?'

Lindsey wanted to indicate that the more information he had, the better the chance that the pattern of events would become visible. 'If you don't mind.'

'She told me that my husband had fettucini alfredo for dinner before he was killed. He ate Italian food. He loved Italy. I know that. She couldn't surprise me. She told me he had just a little alcohol in his blood, but he was not drunk. She told me he had no heroin, cocaine, or marijuana in his blood. She told me he was killed between eleven at night and two o'clock in the morning. She told me the bullet in his belly went right through him and out his back. They found it in the alley. The bullet in his head, it was still in his head when they opened him . . . ' Her face turned green. She lurched to her feet.

Zaffira Fornari reacted faster than Lindsey. She caught her sister by the arms and led her away. From another room Lindsey heard the sound of retching and moaning. Lindsey didn't know what to do. He walked to the window and looked down into the quiet street. The snow lay deep. Darkness had fallen and streetlights had come on. Somewhere in the building someone must have turned on a stereo; he heard an orchestra playing a Christmas carol.

The two sisters reappeared. 'Mr. Lindsey,' Zaffira said.

'Maybe I should go,' he told her. 'Maybe I should come back another day. After, ah . . . '

'The funeral?' Zaffira guided her sister back to her easy chair. She poured tea into three cups.

Ester said, 'Stay, Mr. Lindsey. What can I tell you that will help you? I know you are helping us.'

Lindsey picked up his notebook and pencil. 'Mrs. Berry, you told me that your family disapproved of your marrying Cletus. But how did you get to know him?'

Ester smiled. 'I had a very protected childhood, you understand? I come from a very old, good family. My family thought they were real Italians; they were

97

in Rome for thousands of years. Can you understand thousands of years? In this new country, this new America?'

She lifted her cup and took a sip of tea. There was a dish of little cookies on the silver tray. Lindsey took a cookie and put it down on his saucer beside his cup. 'How did you and Cletus meet?' he asked once more.

'He was a soldier. A warrant officer, you know what that is?'

Lindsey nodded.

'He was part of NATO. They had their big headquarters in Belgium. They had headquarters in other countries, too. We were supposed to be afraid the Russians were coming in their big tanks to crush us, like they did in Prague. That I remember. Yes, sister?'

'I remember,' Zaffira agreed. 'We are little girls then but we remember that.'

'I was seventeen when I met him,' Ester resumed. 'I was in the museum. With my sister — you remember, sister?'

Zaffira said, 'I remember.'

'We were looking at paintings. I thought that the history of the world was

98

best recorded in its art. Paintings, statues, tapestries. We were in the Pinacoteca Capitolina of the Palazzo dei Conservatori. I remember, I was standing in front of a Tintoretto virgin. Wearing schoolgirl uniform. Very modest. You understand, Mr. Lindsey?'

'I understand.'

'And I saw this American soldier in his uniform. I knew the insignia; we used to see British, Dutch, all the uniforms. And this warrant officer came over and spoke to me in very good Italian. He asked if I knew anything about Tintoretto, and I was so frightened of him that I tried to hide behind Zaffira. Do you remember, sister?'

'I remember.'

'Did he follow you home?' Lindsey asked.

'No, nothing as trite as that. I saw him again at a museum. You weren't there, Zaffira. I was there with my friend Veronica Scaletti.' She smiled as she relived the event. 'We went to the Galleria Spada on the Piazza Capo di Ferro. Veronica and I were standing in front of *Saint Cecelia Playing a Lute*. The artist was a woman, did you know that? Artemisia Gentileschi. Women were thought to be good only for bearing children and cooking in those days.'

She paused and sipped at her tea. Then she resumed. 'Veronica and I were talking about Artemisia, when he appeared again. He came over to us. He said he was surprised to see me. He asked if he could buy us an espresso. He loved espresso, you know?'

'That I know,' Lindsey said.

'Cletus was very proper. He took us both for espresso and biscotti. He knew Rome very well, you know.'

Lindsey said, 'No, I didn't know that, or that he'd been in the army.'

'When he came to my house the first time, the whole street buzzed. There were no gentiles on our street. The Piazzetta del Pancotto has been a Jewish street for centuries. Even when the Nazis came, my mother told us, some of the Jews stayed. Others hid, others the Nazis took. The Lazarinis have owned their house in the Piazzetta del Pancotto for so many generations, nobody knows when we first got it.'

Zaffira rose and went to look out of the window behind Ester. Ester said, 'Sister, stop worrying. She's all right.'

'She has to cross the street.'

'She goes to school herself every day. You and I, Zaffira, we were raised in a sheltered world.'

'My husband was not sheltered. Your husband was not sheltered. Let the child be protected.' She rubbed at the window pane. 'There, I see her coming now. With her dog.'

Lindsey said, 'Should I leave, then?'

Ester held out a hand toward him. 'Stay,' she said. 'Take supper with us.'

Lindsey headed for the table. The telephone rang and Zaffira scurried to answer it. He heard her speak in Italian, then call her sister. Ester spoke for a while, then hung up the phone and went into the kitchen.

'Relatives,' Zaffira said. 'Cousins. Aunts and uncles. Our family. My husband, may he rest — his family. They call every hour. They bring food and sit.

I guess they try and help.'

The meal was plain, chicken soup with vegetables and noodles. There was no separate dining room in the apartment, merely an ell off the living room, with the kitchen door just beyond. Anna had gone to her room to wash and change her clothes for dinner. She returned wearing a white T-shirt and jeans. The dog sat in a corner, watching them eat.

Zaffira brought the food from the kitchen. Before anyone touched it, Ester said a prayer in Hebrew. Lindsey had shared evenings with Eric Coffman and his wife Miriam, and their daughters, so the little ceremony did not catch him totally off guard.

He knew that Cletus Berry's funeral was scheduled for the next morning, and he expected to be there; it was International Surety policy. It was also his friend's burial. He thought that Berry's widow and her sister and daughter might prefer to be alone tonight, to prepare themselves for the ordeal. But the two women seemed to be trying to make the evening seem remotely like a normal one,

102

probably for Anna Maria's sake.

'What did you do at Shoshana's house?' Ester asked her.

'She has some new history software she showed me. We looked up Italy and Africa and Israel. We both have to do papers for school. Then we surfed the net for a while. We met some interesting kids and talked about basketball. And one kid who wanted to talk about cooking. Shoshana told him about her dad and that shut him up for good.'

'Fine.' Zaffira ran her hand over her niece's hair. To Lindsey she said, 'Shoshana's father is a chef. A place they call it Pete's Tavern. Downtown. Good food. Not so Italian, but good.'

Anna Maria looked at Lindsey. He'd never seen eyes like this child's. The mixture of genes she'd inherited had harmonized to perfection. He thought, if things had worked out differently — if he and Marvia Plum had ever given Jamie a half-brother or sister — would she be this beautiful and vibrant?

'Mr. Lindsey? Were you really my father's friend?' she asked him.

'Yes, I was. I'd have liked to know him better than I did. What can I tell you, Anna Maria? Or, what can you tell me?'

'Maybe some things,' she said. She turned her attention to her plate.

Ester said, 'Anna Maria is the family historian now. She took that over from me. I went to school with the great Carlo Pacinelli. You don't know him in America, but in school he was my friend. When I was younger I was the family historian, but my daughter is now.'

Anna said, 'Can I show Mr. Lindsey my computer?'

'Finish your meal first.'

'After, then.'

Lindsey said, 'I don't think I should stay late. Tomorrow is — I mean, I thought you might want to — '

'Maybe we should be together. Thank you, Mr. Lindsey.'

Zaffira retired to the kitchen and returned with coffee for the adults and a glass of milk for Anna.

Lindsey wiped his lips on his linen napkin. 'Another time.' He smiled at

Anna. 'Another time, I'd like to see your computer.'

She said, 'My dad bought it for me as a present for my last birthday.'

Lindsey rode down in the elevator, struck by the stray question: What had happened to Zaffira Fornari's husband?

8

Back at the Torrington Tower apartment, Lindsey changed into casuals and then checked his watch. Even allowing for time zones, it was after normal office hours in Denver, but Desmond Richelieu was in the habit of working late. If nothing else, Lindsey could leave a message on Richelieu's voicemail, or email him from his laptop. Or from Cletus Berry's desktop.

The police had checked the contents of Berry's computer, Sokolov had told Lindsey, and found nothing out of the ordinary. But they didn't know International Surety procedure in general or SPUDS in particular. They didn't know SPUDS at all. This was something that Lindsey would look into.

But first he picked up Berry's telephone and punched in the number of Desmond Richelieu's private line. Richelieu recognized Lindsey's voice at

106

once. 'What have you got for me?' He did not mince words. 'You haven't filed a report.'

'I'm not ready.'

'Lindsey, this isn't just a claim. Somebody scragged one of my boys, and I'm damned if I let it slide.'

'I understand, Mr. Richelieu.' Lindsey could see him communing with the autographed portrait of J. Edgar Hoover that hung behind his desk in Denver. 'I've been collecting pieces. They don't make a picture yet. I'm not sure if I'm missing some important piece or if I don't understand what I have.'

'I know how you work, Lindsey. You keep on collecting pieces. I know you'll put it together.' Richelieu shifted gears without pausing for breath. 'What time is the funeral?'

'Tomorrow at eleven.'

'I spoke with Morris Zissler. He ordered flowers, per the manual. He'll pick you up. Where are you staying?'

Lindsey told him.

'You think that's a good idea? We'll spring for a hotel room, Lindsey. What kind of cheapskate outfit do you think we are?'

'It isn't that,' Lindsey demurred. 'I just feel as if I might get something, some idea, pick up some clue by staying here. I mean, Cletus's belongings, his files. I think I just might get something.'

'Okay, Lindsey. You stay with it.' He shifted gear again. 'What kind of cooperation are you getting from the police there?'

Lindsey told Richelieu of his visit to Midtown North and his meeting with Marcie Sokolov.

'Not so good, eh? All right, Lindsey. I don't want you just going through the motions on this thing. I know you won't do that, that's why I gave you this job.'

'He was my friend, Mr. Richelieu.'

'Keep at it. You're a goddamn thorn in my side half the time, too. But you're still my best agent.' Lindsey heard the line go dead. That was Richelieu's style.

He turned to Berry's desktop computer and hit the power switch. He should be able to work with Berry's computer as easily as he did with his own. Even if

Berry had protected his files with passwords, Lindsey had access to SPUDS override coding that should get him through the barriers. Such were the prerogatives of standing near the flagpole.

Time was when Lindsey was a computer illiterate, back in his pre-SPUDS days, when he'd worked out of International Surety's branch office in Walnut Creek, a few miles to the east of Oakland, California. That was his first brush with an authentic, bona fide, no-doubt-about-it genius, M. Martin Saxon. Saxon had turned a startup computer company into a major industry player, sold out, and moved to a farm in Vermont to tinker with circuits and invent software. He'd invited Lindsey to look him up, and Lindsey had agreed to. He'd put Saxon's Vermont address into his pocket organizer and never looked at it again.

Berry's files were pretty conventional. One thing that he'd done was set up a name-and-address file. Lindsey scrolled through it, hoping to find an entry for Alcide Castellini, but there was none. If there was something fishy going on with Castellini, Berry would either have encrypted the entry or simply committed it to memory. Still, Lindsey gave it a shot. He tried word searches for Castellini and Alcide. Nothing. He tried again, using the telephone number that Cele Johnston had given him. *Nada.* Nor was there an entry for Frankie Fulton or for Millicent Martin/Martinelli.

Scrolling through Berry's address file, Lindsey found few surprises, if any. He found himself in the file, as well as Desmond Richelieu, Aurora Delano, half a dozen other SPUDS stalwarts. Moe Zissler at Manhattan East. That was no surprise. And plenty of others that rang no bells with Lindsey. Some of the addresses indicated business connections. Others might be friends; Berry was personable enough to have a huge Christmas card list.

Lindsey was on the verge of giving up when a name caught his attention: Harry Scott. A familiar name; Lindsey could almost identify it. Leaving Berry's address file open, he toggled into KlameNet/Plus and dialed up the SPUDS master directory. There was Harry Scott, SPUDS Regional, southern Europe. It might mean something that Cletus Berry had Scott's addresses — email, snail mail, fax — as well as a Rome telephone number in his personal look-up. Or the man might simply be an old buddy from Berry's army days.

Lindsey closed the file and took a look at Berry's directory. The biggest part of his records was given over to case files, sequenced by IS policy number. He started through Berry's personal case files. Most of the cases were as close to routine as SPUDS cases ever got. He came across an entry for one of his own cases, the MacReedy death claim on which Berry had ferreted out a sixty-year-old copy of the *Mosholu Parkway Jewish Community Center Bulletin* and relayed its contents to Lindsey. That information had helped Lindsey to unravel a bizarre and complicated puzzle. But aside from the MacReedy case, and a few others that Lindsey had had a fleeting connection with, or that Berry had told him about at one of the periodic SPUDS conferences they both attended, nothing looked familiar and everything looked kosher.

Except for one oddity.

The case numbers were eight digits long. If you knew the coding you could easily tell whether the claim had been filed against International Surety or one of the predecessor companies that had amalgamated decades ago to form IS. And you could tell the year the policy was issued, the year the claim was filed, the status of the claim, and year it was paid out if it had been paid. Most of Berry's cases came on IS files, since the claims had been filed no earlier than 1981. But here was a peculiar one. The issuing company was the New York Amalgamated Guarantee Insurance Company. Lindsey had seen occasional references to the company. Global National and New York Amalgamated had been affiliated long before they disappeared into International Surety. They even had nicknames: *Gingle* and *Nyagic*. They rhymed with single and tragic.

The MacReedy case had involved a

Gingle policy. And the Nyagic case that Lindsey had found in Berry's records had an issue date of 1938. A claim had been filed against the policy in 1940. And the claim had been paid and the case marked closed in 1951.

Why had it taken eleven years to pay the claim? And why did Berry have a copy of the file on his hard disk when he hadn't joined IS until 1981?

Lindsey hit the familiar sequence of keys that would open the case file for him, and nothing happened. He tried again. Access was denied.

He logged onto Klamenet/Plus. His top-level SPUDS clearance should get him anything he wanted outside of top-level, personal-and-confidential corporate files. He keyed in the odd seven-digit policy number and drew a blank. It just wasn't in the International Surety master file.

Lindsey's clearance got him into an ancient New York Amalgamated Guarantee directory. He keyed in the file number for the 1938 policy, but again he drew a blank.

He bailed out of KNP and scooted Cletus Berry's swivel chair over to the closet, fished his pocket organizer out of his suit jacket, and looked up M. Martin Saxon. There he was, snugged away in the bosom of Bellows Falls, Vermont. He'd given Lindsey both a telephone number and an online address as well as his mailing address. If only they were still valid . . . It had been half a decade; in the electronic world, that was more like half a millennium.

Lindsey composed an email and zapped it off to Saxon. He didn't have to wait long for a reply. He guessed that Saxon must spend a lot of time online.

Nice to hear from you. Wondered whatever became of you and those comic books. What are you up to?

What *was* he up to? Lindsey sketched out his problem with the New York Amalgamated policy. When Saxon's reply appeared on the monitor screen, Lindsey could almost hear the laughter.

You corporate types and your security coding. I guess you'll never learn that there's no lock without a key. Even if you

114

can't open the file, see if you can upload it and zap it to me.

Showing IS policies to outsiders was a breach of confidentiality, unless the policy-holder gave permission. But in this case, there was no way to get that permission.

Somewhere, Joseph Heller was laughing up his sleeve.

Lindsey explained the problem to Saxon. A message came back.

Pay me one dollar. Hire me as a consultant. I'll sign a confidential disclosure agreement.

A couple more messages and they'd settled. It was only a virtual dollar, of course, but then it was only a virtual signature. Lindsey figured they were equally real. He uploaded the Nyagic file and zapped it to Saxon. Saxon sent a message back.

Go walk around the block. Enjoy nature. This is going to take a little while.

Lindsey phoned Moe Zissler instead. Yes, Zissler had ordered flowers for Cletus Berry's funeral, and he was planning to attend the service and the burial, as per company policy. Of course he'd pick Lindsey up at 58th Street and they could ride together.

Lindsey lay down on top of the futon, comfortable in his sweats. He was half-dozing when Berry's computer sounded a chime.

Piece of cake. I only read the heading on the file to make sure I'd cracked it. Then I wiped it. Your secrets are safe with me. Attached coding will do the trick for you. First line will tell you how to install it. Call me any time. That buck will come in handy.

Lindsey downloaded the code and followed Saxon's instructions for install-ing it on Berry's desktop. Then he crossed his fingers and hit the Nyagic file with Saxon's code. It opened with a pop he could almost hear.

The first thing Lindsey looked for was the name of the policy-holder. The policy had been issued in the name of His Majesty Victor Emmanuel III, King of Italy and Sardinia.

He logged onto KlameNet/Plus and put the Nyagic file back into International

Surety's database. He didn't know who had erased it, although Cletus Berry had to be a prime candidate for that little caper.

He logged off KNP, brought the file back up, and leaned back in his chair. At least Berry had a good big monitor with nice bright phosphors. Still, it was going to be a long night.

9

Lindsey hated the service at the funeral home on the Upper West Side, in which he stood between Moe Zissler and the grieving women, listening to the sound of crying. He wore the black tie he'd brought with him from Denver. He'd brought the tie as a symbol of — something.

Ester Berry, Zaffira Fornari, and Anna Maria were a mass of blackness. The two women kept the little girl between them, as if to protect her from the reality of the event. A broad-shouldered man was standing with them, touching the women's shoulders and murmuring to them; stroking the child's hair as if he were petting a nervous colt. Anna Maria took his hand between hers and held his palm over her eyes.

Lindsey caught a glimpse of skin on Ester's shoulder. He peered at her, then at Zaffira and Anna Maria. Each of them had opened a seam at the shoulder of her dress. The broad-shouldered man wore a small black ribbon pinned to his lapel. It had been cut partway through, and the lower half hung at a crooked angle.

The service was Jewish. More Eric Coffman data. The opened seams were symbolic of the mourners rending their clothing in anguish. The sliced black ribbon represented a heart torn by grief. Berry has never mentioned religion to Lindsey, and Lindsey had got the impression that Berry was indifferent to the subject. Whatever got the mourners through the ordeal, Lindsey thought. Cletus Berry didn't care.

The congregation was equally mixed, black and white. No one talked much except the rabbi. He referred to 'the deceased.' Not Mr. Berry, not Cletus. The deceased. And the bereaved wife of the deceased, dear Ester, and the bereaved daughter of the deceased, dear Anna Maria, and the bereaved brother of the deceased, dear Petrus.

Dear Petrus. At least Lindsey knew who the broad-shouldered black man was, and why he'd looked so familiar. Lindsey had never known that Cletus Berry had a brother.

The rabbi delivered a eulogy. When the service ended and they filed out of the funeral home for the ride to the cemetery, Lindsey spotted another familiar figure: Marcie Sokolov. She nodded to him, then slipped out the door. They rode in a heated car across one of the city's bridges to Queens, and to the cemetery.

Zissler asked Lindsey how he liked New York. He let his gaze wander. The city looked gray and dingy; the day was cold and bleak. He shrugged. 'Maybe it's more fun in the spring.'

At the cemetery they gathered around the grave. Lindsey shuddered. It was hard to accept the reality of the scene. Everything was cliché — the mourners, their breath rising in columns of steam; the murmured conversations; the sobs. Ester and Zaffira had made a shelter of themselves for Anna Maria. Marcie Sokolov stood a few yards away, her eyes darting from person to person. The hearse arrived last, preceded by the rabbi's car.

There were a few folding chairs. A funeral director led Ester, Zaffira and Anna Maria to them and urged them to be seated. All the mourners ranged themselves near the grave, save for one who stood near a limousine. Lindsey got one clear glimpse of the man: silver hair, distinguished, handsome face; stocky build; fiftyish. It was Alcide Castellini.

The rabbi was praying in Hebrew. The *kaddish*, Lindsey remembered. Some of the mourners followed, also in Hebrew. Ester and Zaffira mixed sobs with words Lindsey didn't understand; the little girl only cried.

Lindsey watched Petrus Berry advance and put his arms around the three of them, dipping his head to the level of the women's faces. Lindsey could see the two women nodding. The man reached between them to take Anna Maria away from the graveside but she dug her heels into the frozen earth, refusing to go. The man stopped tugging and remained with the family.

The casket was lowered and the ceremonial handfuls of dirt were thrown onto it. The three shrouded females walked to the limousine, Petrus Berry with them, managing somehow to keep them encircled in his arms. A driver opened the limousine door. Before he could close it, the rabbi made his way to the limousine, spoke briefly with the family of the dear deceased, then turned away. The driver closed the passenger door, climbed into the driver's seat, and slammed his own door.

The procession began to move from the cemetery, the tires of the vehicles crunching on the gravel-covered blacktop. Lindsey blew a cloud of breath into the air, feeling like an extra in a Hammer horror film save for the icy fist clutching his heart. He looked around for Alcide Castellini, who was nowhere to be seen. Then he spotted Moe Zissler. Lindsey heaved a sigh and headed for him, ready to return to Manhattan, but he was halted by a hand clutching his biceps. He turned and saw Marcie Sokolov.

'We've got something.'

'That's . . . ' For a moment Lindsey was stymied. He'd thought the police had just been going through the motions.

'You can come over to the shop this afternoon if you feel like it. Phone first, so I won't be out. But I think I can show you something good.'

That was all Lindsey could get out of her. He rode back to 58th Street with Zissler. As the Buick curved down an off-ramp, Zissler asked, 'Do you want to come up and look around Manhattan East?'

'No thanks, Moe. Just drop me at Seventh Avenue and I'll go on from there.'

'Okay.'

At length Zissler pulled the Buick to the curb and Lindsey opened the door and got out. He stopped for a salad and a cup of tea, then walked the cold city sidewalks back to the Torrington Tower. He waved to Lou Halter, back on duty and sitting like a fixture at the desk in his gray guard's uniform, then rode up in the elevator and entered Cletus Berry's private digs.

123

Once inside, Lindsey laid Congressman Amoroso's campaign brochure on the desk beside Cletus Berry's computer, then pulled the Nyagic file up and displayed it on the monitor once more. He scrolled through the file, then checked the credit-line on the brochure, picked up Berry's telephone, and dialed directory assistance. A few minutes later he heard the buzzing of a telephone ringing in New Haven, Connecticut. He hoped that William Van Huysen was home, and that he'd be willing to talk with him.

A child answered the phone and Lindsey asked if Dr. Van Huysen was there. He heard the child put the phone down and summon the professor. It was winter break at Yale University, and Lindsey offered up a breath of thanks that Van Huysen had not left town when the students did.

'I just read your little essay in Congressman Amoroso's campaign bro- chure,' Lindsey began when Van Huysen picked up the phone.

Van Huysen stopped him right there. 'I'm sorry about that. I thought Amoroso was getting up a little educational pamphlet. I didn't know it was for a piece of campaign literature. I am not a political person and I don't want to get involved with politics.'

Lindsey said, 'No, I'm not political either. I'm in the insurance business. I was up all last night, studying an old case file, and — '

'What did you say your name was?'

'Hobart Lindsey. I'm associated with International Surety. Perhaps you've heard of us.'

'What was that about an old case?' Van Huysen spoke in a bland, droning voice.

'Your essay about the Silver Chariot, Dr. Van Huysen.'

'Yes. Caesar's Chariot.'

'Was it really Caesar's?'

'I don't know.' Van Huysen heaved a sigh. 'Look, Mr. Lindsey, I've work to attend to over this holiday break. What is it, precisely, that you want from me?'

'Well, your essay about the chariot says that it disappeared in 1940. Can you tell me about that? In any more detail, I mean.'

'Mr. Lindsey, you'd better tell me exactly what this is all about before I answer any more questions for you.'

'It's rather complicated, Professor.'

'Well, frankly, I don't like dealing over the telephone. Is this something that your company needs to know? Are you trying to settle a claim, or what?'

'Not really. One of our employees — a frend of mine — was murdered, you see. so I really have both a personal and an official interest in justice. The police have the case, but I'm not really confident that they're handling it effectively. So I'm trying to gather some information myself.'

'I'll tell you what,' Van Huysen said. 'If your corporation wants to pick my brain, they can hire me as a consultant. Pay my fee, you come on up here to New Haven, and I'll be happy to answer your questions.'

'I'm sure we can arrange that,' Lindsey consented. 'How about tomorrow?'

Tomorrow it was. Van Huysen named a fee and Lindsey agreed. It was nice having the authority to commit International Surety to an expenditure without fighting the corporate bureaucracy.

Next he telephoned Marcie Sokolov and made an appointment to visit her at Midtown North later that afternoon. Then he put on his overcoat and left the building. The city's lovely covering of snow had turned to filthy slush; it hadn't taken long for that to happen.

Inside the lobby of the police station, Lindsey picked up a visitor's badge and made his way to Detective Sokolov. Sokolov looked up at him and smiled. 'You're still pushing on this, aren't you?'

'Not quitting, no.'

Sokolov nodded to a hard chair and Lindsey lowered himself into it. He said, 'I guess I have a different view of this murder than you do, Detective. I think Berry was killed for a reason, and I think I'm starting to get a handle on that reason.'

'Really?' She rested her elbows on her desk and laced her fingers under her chin.

'I think Cletus knew Frankie Fulton.'

'So do I.'

'And I've been following a chain that led from Frankie Fulton to a dead showgirl named Millicent Martin. And from her to an antiques dealer named Alcide Castellini.'

Sokolov leaned back in her chair. 'Really, Mr. Lindsey. And what is the connection between all these people, and why would Alcide Castellini want to kill Cletus Berry?'

Lindsey shook his head. 'I didn't say Castellini killed Berry. I just said that the chain led to him. Link by link. I don't know whether it ends with Castellini or whether there are more links. But I'm going to find out, even if the NYPD isn't interested.'

Sokolov smiled broadly. 'So the determined amateur is going to show up the professionals again, is he? I submit, sir, that you've been watching too much TV.'

Lindsey watched as she stood up and carried a manila folder from her desk to a copier. She ran a couple of sheets of paper through the machine and handed a copy of one to him. 'Take a look, Mr. Lindsey. That's a composite sketch by our best artist. Look familiar to you?'

Lindsey studied the artist's rendering of a young Asian man wearing a knitted watch cap. His face was thin, his skin stretched tight over protruding cheek-bones. He had a large wart on one side of his jaw.

'Doesn't look even remotely like anybody I can think of.'

'No luck, eh? All right. Look at this.' She handed him a second sheet of paper. This one was a photocopy of a regular photographic print. It was presumably a police records photo of the man in the sketch.

Lindsey asked, 'Who is this?'

'Low-budget hit-man named Johnny Thieu Ng. Parents were boat people. Johnny was born here, grew up in Vietnamese gangs, graduated into the mainstream after a couple of shoot-outs between Asian and Anglo mobs. If you can't beat 'em, hire 'em.'

Lindsey raised a picture in each hand, looking from one to the other. 'You think this man killed Berry and Fulton?'

'We've got an eye witness.'

'Who is it?'

'I don't think you'd know him, and I wouldn't tell you anyway. He's a good source. He's helped us on a number of cases. If we let his identity out he'd lose his usefulness to us.'

'But how did — '

'He saw the killing. He says he was out for a walk — '

'A *walk*? In December, on a freezing cold night?'

Sokolov grinned. 'That's his story and he's sticking with it, Mr. Amateur. He was out for a walk, he heard a quarrel, he thought a citizen might be getting mugged so he raced to the rescue. And his timeline jibes with the coroner's estimated time of death. Right smack in the middle, in fact.'

'Oh, please.' Lindsey shook his head.

'He heard a series of shots and ran to assist the victims. If he couldn't prevent the tragedy, perhaps he could render emergency first aid. As he entered the alley he saw a man run out with a pistol in his hand. He bent over the victims but saw that they had both expired. What to do? He turned and pursued the perpetrator but he slipped on a patch of icy sidewalk. He fell and hit his head. He was stunned. He lost his memory of what he'd just seen, but when he heard a broadcast offering a reward — ' She smiled again. 'Well.' She spread her hands on her desk. 'Our good citizen was jolted into remembering, and came right in and told us what he'd seen, and asked for his usual finder's fee plus the reward money. Isn't that wonderful, Mr. Lindsey? So now maybe you'll just go back to Aspen — '

'Denver.'

' — and let us do our jobs.'

Lindsey looked at the sketch and the photograph. 'You matched the drawing to a mug shot?'

'In a flash.'

'And you've picked up Ng?'

'We've put out an order.'

'And you think that's the end of the case?'

'What do you think?'

'I think its the biggest pile of baloney I've ever heard.'

'Pile of baloney?' Sokolov chuckled. 'I

like that. What pre-school did you pick that up from, Mr. Lindsey?'

Lindsey asked if he could keep the pictures. Sokolov said he could. He remembered to leave his visitor's badge behind when he left the building.

10

Walking into Grand Central had been like walking into a movie. Lindsey expected to see Cary Grant or Myrna Loy appear at any moment. He bought his round-trip ticket to New Haven, drank a cup of coffee while he waited for the gate to open, and climbed aboard a coach.

He was traveling against the rush, so he had no trouble finding a window seat and settling in. He opened his laptop and booted up the Nyagic file. He knew what he wanted to ask Professor Van Huysen, but he wanted to review the case once more before they met.

He looked around and discovered that the passengers were divided almost evenly between those working with laptops and those wearing earphones, sitting with their eyes closed, zoned out listening to whatever people listened to on those gadgets.

The policy was written in the name of

the King of Italy and Sardinia, but that was obviously a matter of form. The real policy-holder was the Italian government. In 1938 that would have been Benito Mussolini's fascist gang.

Why would New York Amalgamated have sold a policy to that outfit? Lindsey had wondered when he first read the file. The answer was obvious, and it was no different now than it had been six decades ago. But what was insured?

Lindsey probed deeper into the documentation. Ah! The policy actually covered the Italian Pavilion at the New York World's Fair of 1939. The building itself, furniture and equipment, the staff, exhibits, possible injuries to visitors . . . It all looked pretty routine.

There was an appendix, also standard in such policies. It was an inventory of furnishings and exhibits: desks, chairs, office machines, and the items on exhibit. These included industrial machinery and munitions, symbols of the might of *Il Duce*'s New Rome.

The New Rome. A vision like Randolph Amoroso's.

But there was a bow to the Old Rome as well, and to the Italy of the Renaissance and the Risorgiamento. Paintings by Correggio and Titian, Giotto and Raphael, even a da Vinci. Sculptures by Cellini, Donatello, Michelangelo Buonarotti. And a separate category for toys — or rather, for a single toy.

Chariot, silver and ironwood, drawn by two horses, one of black marble and one of white marble. Craftsman unknown. Date of manufacture unknown. Dimensions approx. .7 metre length x .2 metre width x .3 metre height. Mounted on black marble base. Weight approx. 10.5 kilogrammes.
Alleged to have been childhood plaything of Julius Caesar.
Value $5 million (US).
Julius Caesar's Silver Chariot.

The Italian Pavilion at the Fair had been inventoried by the Nyagic agent and everything in the inventory was in place. The agent had even hired a couple of authorities in the field to accompany him and authenticate the antiquities and art treasures. *No c'era problema.*

The first season of the fair had been a success. Lindsey knew that; he'd seen a PBS documentary about it. But the Second World War broke out in September of that year, and by the time the fair reopened for its 1940 season, half the exhibiting nations were either at war or already defeated by Hitler's armies, and their pavilions remained closed. Whatever could be transported back to Europe was loaded onto ships and sent home. The rest was sold for salvage or simply scrapped. The Italians had packed everything carefully in padded crates, loaded their treasures on board the *Fior di Rimini*, and sent them back to the museums of Rome and Florence.

Did Nyagic care? You bet it did! And when every statue and painting and suit of Roman armor and ancient coin and medieval manuscript was unpacked and safely signed for, a sigh of relief must have gone up that Lindsey could still hear, echoing across the decades.

Every statue and every painting and

every suit of Roman armor. But not Julius Caesar's Silver Chariot with its two marble horses.

The chariot had been the centerpiece of *Il Duce*'s exhibit, and it had taken a packing crate the size and shape of an elaborate coffin to protect it. Even then, the file indicated, the *Fior di Rimini* had carried a staff of curators whose sole duty aboard ship was to monitor the artworks and antiquities and make sure that nothing happened to any of them.

But something *had* happened. When the returning crates were inventoried on the dock at La Spezia, prior to transshipment to Rome, everything seemed to be in order. Not so with the curators. One of them, *Dottore* Massimo di Verolini of the University of Rome, could not be accounted for.

The fascist authorities panicked. A bureaucrat named Salvatore Castellini was sent up from Rome to sniff around. Literally. One of the crates drew his attention, due to the very peculiar odor coming from it. Castellini wasn't a professional curator, he was a fascist party hack who had worn a black shirt and marched on Rome with Mussolini and clubbed Communists and Socialists and liberals and everybody else who got in *Il Duce*'s path. He ordered the crates opened, and . . .

And when the crates were opened, every painting and every medieval manuscript, every ancient coin and every elaborately worked goblet, was safe and unscathed.

Except for Caesar's chariot.

The coffin-sized and coffin-shaped packing crate that was supposed to yield up the beautiful silver-and-marble miniature contained instead the remains of *Dottore* di Verolini. The *Dottore* had been dead for several days, the hold of *Fior di Rimini* was warm and unventilated, and the remains were ripening very nicely.

But the body was not so far gone that a hastily organized autopsy failed to determine the cause of death. *Dottore* di Verolini had been attacked from the rear; that was obvious. His skull had been crushed with the proverbial heavy instrument. But this time it was not blunt; it

138

had had a sharp corner. The victim had apparently died at once.

When and where had the crime been committed? It was impossible to tell. Possibly in New York, before the *Fior di Rimini* had even set sail. Or possibly while the ship was en route from New York to the port of La Spezia. In any case, the victim's body was returned to his family and buried with all due dispatch.

What heavy blunt instrument had been used? The chariot, complete with horses and base, had weighed 10.5 kilogrammes — well over 20 pounds. The base probably had sharp edges. It would make a somewhat clumsy murder weapon, but obviously an effective one.

The chariot was missing, of course. It was never seen again.

★ ★ ★

Lindsey looked up from the laptop computer screen and blinked. A grim winter landscape whizzed past the car's grimy windows. He closed the laptop and walked the length of the car, carrying the computer with him. Suddenly the world was not to be trusted.

He stood on the platform between passenger coaches, watching the Connecticut landscape roll by and wondering if there was any connection between Salvatore Castellini the fascist party hack and Alcide Castellini the silver-haired antique dealer. Was the name Castellini the Italian equivalent of Smith or Jones? Or . . .

At length Lindsey returned to his seat, feeling refreshed, and reopened the Nyagic file. The King of Italy had filed two claims against New York Amalgamated: one for the death of Massimo di Verolini, one for the loss of the Silver Chariot. The di Verolini claim was in the amount of $15,000 — a sizable sum in 1940. The claim for the lost chariot was, yes, in the amount of $5,000,000.

Apparently a check had gone out to the King of Italy for $15,000. Lindsey could only hope that it had somehow reached *Dottore* di Verolini's family and not gone into the coffers of Benito Mussolini's fascist war machine. But that was chicken feed compared to the claim for the missing chariot. And it looked as if Uncle Sam had stepped in and done a little arm-twisting at New York Amalgamated, to get the company to stall that payment. The file was conspicuously vague about that. Maybe something had been lost in transition from paper to microfilm to mylar-coated disk, or maybe someone had gone in and sanitized the record somewhere along the way. But it looked as if the government had encouraged Nyagic to route the claim through a corporate maze, lose a few papers and ask the claimant to refile them, send documents back for clarification or notarization, or whatever it took to keep from shelling out. And Lindsey knew well that insurance companies could find reasons to delay shelling out large payments.

Before the money moved, the US was in World War II, Italy was an enemy nation, and the Silver Chariot claim was in limbo. When the war ended, Italy was an occupied country with a provisional government. Mussolini was dead, Victor

Emmanuel was still on the throne, and a referendum was in the works. The chariot had never turned up, but Italy was in shambles, as was most of Europe. Nazi *Gauleiters* had stolen hundreds of millions of dollars' worth of art treasures in occupied countries, including Italy after the fall of Mussolini and the surrender of his successors to the Allies.

Victor Emmanuel lost the referendum. Italy became a republic. The new government reinstated the claim against New York Amalgamated — only to learn that that company had become part of International Surety. And to discover that the 1940 claim filed by the King of Italy and Sardinia was still on file. If the $5,000,000 was to be paid out, to whom would it be paid? The new government of the Republic of Italy, or the King, now the ex-King, living in comfortable exile with a flock of other royal has-beens, never-weres, and hoped-to-bes, on the Riviera?

Lindsey looked up again. The conductor had announced that the train was approaching New Haven. Outside the window, the ramshackle tenements and decrepit industrial buildings that lined the tracks were growing more dense.

There was just time to finish reading the file. The official Nyagic and IS documents were straightforward enough, but somebody had added a historical commentary that set the events in context. An Italian politician named Alcide de Gasperi had served in the provisional government under the occupation, and when the republic got on its feet, he became premier. Initially, de Gasperi's government was a coalition that included the Italian Communist Party, headed by Palmiro Togliatti.

The communists were beholden to Moscow. They made no secret of their intention of taking full control of the government and swinging Italy into the Soviet orbit. The Cold War was in its early stages, and the US government was beside itself at the prospect of a communist Italy. In 1947, with American encouragement and support, de Gasperi broke with Togliatti, throwing the communists out of his coalition. But the communists were the largest single party in Italy, and without them in his coalition, de Gasperi's government collapsed. He had no choice but to call for elections, and at that point Uncle Sam gave International Surety a gentle nudge.

International Surety had run into some tax problems as the result of its takeover of Global International and New York Amalgamated. And Uncle Sam dropped a none-too-subtle hint that things would go a lot better for International Surety if the old Silver Chariot claim was paid out — with interest — to the de Gasperi government.

It had been. And de Gasperi had won the election, using International Surety's millions for campaign funds. And the world had been saved for free enterprise and democracy.

Fifty years later, the Silver Chariot file had mysteriously disappeared from International Surety's database, and turned up under electronic lock and key in Cletus Berry's desktop computer.

And Berry had served in the United States army in Italy in the 1970s.

And now Cletus Berry was dead.

Curiouser . . . and curiouser.

★　★　★

William Van Huysen met Lindsey at the railroad station near downtown New Haven. At Van Huysen's suggestion, they climbed into his Jaguar XJ-6. Van Huysen said, 'So you want to know about my little essay for Congressman Amoroso, is that it? You looking for some dirt on Randolph? I'm afraid you've wasted a trip if that's what you're after.'

'Not exactly. I'm not interested in Amoroso. I'm interested in the chariot itself.'

Van Huysen grunted. He eased the Jaguar to a stop behind a huge, mud-splattered delivery truck. 'Say, have you eaten lunch yet? I don't imagine they gave you much on that train.'

Lindsey realized that he'd had nothing since breakfast. He said so.

'How about a cozy campus hang-out?'

'Whatever.'

Van Huysen maneuvered the Jaguar

through openings in the traffic like a fencer driving a foil through an opponent's defense. His choice turned out to be off campus, a bustling bar and restaurant decorated with an eclectic mix of sports memorabilia and Irish patriotic symbols. The front window was fogged from the inside and rimed from the outside; green letters edged in gold identified it as Kelly's Chop House and Saloon.

They wound up in a wooden booth under a photo-mural of the 1949 Yale-Princeton football game. A beefy waitress in a peasant blouse asked if they'd like a drink and Van Huysen ordered an Irish whiskey, neat. Lindsey blinked and asked for his with caffeine. The waitress laughed and slapped him on the shoulder. To Van Huysen she said, 'I like your friend, William. You ought to bring him around more often.' She went off to fetch their drinks.

Lindsey got his first good look at William Van Huysen. The man could be anywhere between forty and fifty. His hair was a metallic gray, beautifully trimmed.

His face looked as if he visited a tanning salon regularly.

The waitress brought their drinks and Van Huysen said, 'We'll order our food in a little while.' She went away. He said to Lindsey, 'The meter is running.'

Lindsey laid out his story for Van Huysen. He'd already touched on Berry's death, and his own interest in the case, during their telephone conversation. Now he gave Van Huysen a fuller version. A fuller version, but one that was slightly edited. Van Huysen wasn't entitled to know everything that Lindsey did, and Lindsey wasn't going to tell him more than he thought Van Huysen needed.

In a nutshell, Lindsey had taken over the case load of an IS colleague who had recently died. Most of the inherited files were strictly routine, but one of them involved an old claim arising from the loss of the Silver Chariot as it was being shipped back to Italy from the New York World's Fair. Could Van Huysen give Lindsey some more background on the chariot, so he could figure out just what the odd case was all about?

When Lindsey finished, Van Huysen signaled to the waitress. 'Another round. And a green salad for me. Lindsey?'

Lindsey ordered a bowl of chowder.

11

Van Huysen toyed with his salad as he told the story. The chariot was real. It existed, or at least had existed, as recently as 1940. Lindsey's information about its place in the Italian Pavilion was accurate, and there was ample documentation to support that. On the other hand, if the chariot had indeed been returned to Italy on the *Fior di Rimini*, it might have been destroyed in the carnage of the next five years. Or the chariot might never have been loaded on the *Fior di Rimini*, and might still be somewhere in the United States. Somewhere in some obscure museum, or more likely, carefully locked away in some private collector's personal treasure trove. Collectors were odd ducks, and some of them were fanatics. That, Lindsey already knew. All too well.

'The origins of the Silver Chariot are lost in antiquity,' Van Huysen told

Lindsey. 'Nobody knows how old it is, or who made it.'

'Can't they tell by the style of carving? Or — what, carbon-dating?'

'You can't carbon-date silver, Lindsey. Or marble.'

'The wood, then. The description in our insurance file says that it's made partly of ironwood.'

Van Huysen snorted. 'First of all, there's no such thing as ironwood; that's just a term for any kind of hardwood. My guess would be that the wooden parts of the chariot — the axle and wheel spokes — are made of olive wood, or maybe cedar. And it would be a desecration of the chariot to take even a shaving of the wood to test.'

He signaled the waitress, asked Lindsey with a gesture if he wanted another beverage, relayed the information, and continued his lecture. 'That's all moot anyway, isn't it? There's no chariot to test.'

'But there are pictures. There's one on the Amoroso pamphlet. There's one on his campaign button.'

'And they're probably quite accurate.'

'You're sure of that?'

'Epstein knows more about pictures than I do.'

Lindsey winced. 'Who's Epstein?'

'He's an archaeologist.'

'So come on, help me with this.'

Van Huysen sighed. 'Congressman Amoroso's people came to Epstein first for help. He's the outstanding man in the field, but he's an archaeologist.' He almost spat the last word. 'An archaeologist would deal with artifacts. I'm a classicist. My work is mainly in texts. Original texts — Greek, Latin, Hebrew, Aramaic. But Epstein wouldn't touch it. He told Amoroso's representative to get a classicist or an historian. Finally, Epstein gave them my name and the arrangement was made.'

Lindsey nodded. All right, back to the main topic. 'Didn't, ah, the design of chariots change? Sometimes you can tell what century a ship is from, or a piece of clothing or even a painting.'

Van Huysen accepted another whiskey from the waitress. 'You can indeed,' he agreed. 'But the chariot may have been modified. In fact, there are some old pictures — we can't be sure that they're pictures of *this* chariot, but we think they are — and it looks rather different. These are not photographs, you understand. A toy chariot turns up in an old drawing or painting. It's the artist's vision of the chariot. Was it the same toy? We have to consider how the artist viewed the object as well as what the object actually looked like.'

Van Huysen pushed aside his almost-empty salad dish and it disappeared from the table. 'Now, why would the chariot look different at different times?' he asked. 'Do you know the story of the Roman trireme?'

Lindsey shook his head.

'A Roman merchant owned a trireme. Every time the ship was outfitted for a sea voyage, the merchant had the hull and the decks and oars and all the other parts checked, and anything that was showing signs of wear or rot was replaced. Eventually every part of the ship had been replaced.' He grinned at Lindsey.

'Question: Was it the same ship, or a different one?'

'Of course it was the same ship. Just because the merchant replaced some planks — '

'Not *some* planks, Lindsey. *All* the planks. Everything. There was not one nail or shred or splinter left from the original ship. How could it be the same ship? We don't know if parts of the chariot have been replaced over the years. It *was* a toy, don't you see. One generation's cheap toy, the next generation's valuable antique, another age's priceless art treasure.'

Lindsey shook his head. 'You're telling me you don't know how old this chariot is or who made it or — or anything about it. How could you write that pamphlet?'

'Do you have a copy of my little essay, Lindsey?'

Lindsey produced the pamphlet.

Van Huysen quoted himself: ' 'Its origins are shrouded in mystery. Legend has it that King David ordered it created as a plaything for his son Solomon.' I should think that's clear enough.

Shrouded in mystery . . . legend has it . . . No responsible scholar could say more than that. Maybe the chariot was made in Atlantis. Maybe it was left behind by visiting Martians. We can speculate, but we should try to keep our speculations within reason. And we should label them clearly for what they are. I assure you, I was well aware of that when I wrote the essay for Congressman Amoroso.'

Lindsey leaned his forehead against his hand. 'All right. First, give me the history of the chariot as best you can, speculation or no, legend or no. All right? Second, tell me where you think it is now, to the best of your ability. And third, why is it important? Why would my colleague have had the file on it in a collection of cases that otherwise are all either current or recent? It doesn't make sense to me.'

'Very well. As long as you understand that most of this is a mixture of folklore and speculation. David and Solomon was admittedly stretching a bit. But the Hebrew letters *chet yod* appear to have been worked into the silver. At least, they appear on some images of the chariot. They are the eighth and tenth letters of the alphabet and total eighteen, a very important number in Hebrew tradition. Together they spell *chai*, or life. To say that they mean good luck would be an oversimplification, but they might appear on such a gift from a father to a son.'

Lindsey said, 'I didn't know that Hebrew letters and numbers meant so much.'

Van Huysen leaned back in the booth and smiled. 'Very clever people, the Hebrews. Some of the world's great minds. But there's a streak of primitive superstition, too. They have a prayer or blessing of God, the *chalel*, that they say eighteen times a year. They light candles eighteen minutes before sundown. They have to put their matzos in the oven no more than eighteen minutes after they mix the flour and water. They believe in thirty-six secret saints — double eighteen. The most powerful name of God has seventy-two letters — quadruple eighteen. Heh! Superstition isn't the word for it.' He sipped his drink.

'After David's time,' Van Huysen continued, 'the chariot disappears, then reappears — according to legend — in the court of Philip of Macedon. Again it's a plaything for a royal prince; this time, Alexander the Great. After Alexander's death the chariot disappears for more than 200 years, turning up in the household of Senator Gaius Caesar and his dear wife Aurelia and their three darling children — Julia Prima, Julius, and Julia Secunda. The Romans did not display great imagination in naming their children.' He chuckled at his witticism.

Lindsey admitted that he had never heard of Julius Caesar's two sisters.

'Alas,' Van Huysen sighed, 'so few have. At any rate, the Caesars were a pretty old and successful family in Rome, but their fortunes had been declining gently for a century or so by the time of little Julius's childhood. But the family were still quite influential, and in Rome, politics was all. Gaius Caesar still had some worthwhile clients, and the chariot may have made another appearance in the sack of Corinth in the year 146 before the common era.'

He looked at his whiskey glass. 'Maybe this is more detail than you really need, Lindsey. But if the chariot had been in Corinth since Alexander's time, somehow it made its way to Rome. It may have come with the doctor who delivered little Julius. Caesarian sections are not so-called for nothing. The best Roman doctors were Greeks, and a dispropor-tionate number of them were Hebrews. I guess that the chariot might have fallen on hard times. Some Roman scavenger or junk dealer got his hands on it, saw the *chet yod*, gave it or more likely sold it to a Jewish doctor, and the rest, as they say, is history.'

Van Huysen pushed himself erect and made his way unsteadily to the restroom. As soon as he was out of earshot, Lindsey signaled to the waitress and asked if it would be safe for Van Huysen to drive home. She assured Lindsey that Van Huysen was a valued regular at Kelly's and she would drive him home. Not for the first time.

Van Huysen managed to finish his story

with just a few slurred words. After Caesar's assassination, the toy disappeared again, this time for almost 800 years, turning up as a gift — source not known — to the infant Charlemagne. And then, Van Huysen told Lindsey, the story really got crazy. 'Did Ivan the Great play with the toy? Did Suleiman the Magnificent? The Emperor Joseph of Austria? Nobody knows. From what I've seen of the chariot — twentieth-century photographs — the great Benvenuto Cellini may have refurbished the metalwork. That would be in the sixteenth century. But who knows? Cellini left an autobiography, in which there are some ambivalent references to minor projects. What Cellini considered minor projects.' He shook his head.

'All we know is that Mussolini set great store by the chariot. He almost refused to let the chariot be sent to the World's Fair in 1939, but he finally decided that the glory of the New Rome would shine across the world. You know, he came to power in 1922. He was Adolf's senior partner at first. Then Hitler started to outshine *Il Duce*, and Mussolini wanted to get the spotlight back.'

Lindsey nodded. 'And that's very nearly the end of story, I suppose.'

'Very nearly. The chariot was at the fair. It was supposed to return to Italy. It disappeared. And you know what happened to Mussolini. He shouldn't have let it out of his sight. Oh, well.'

Lindsey said, 'I guess that's about all I need.'

The waitress conferred briefly with the bartender, then returned and rumpled Van Huysen's iron-gray hair with her fingers. She nodded to Lindsey and said, 'Help me with William, will you?'

They got Van Huysen to his feet and started him toward the door. Nobody had paid for the meal or the drinks, but Van Huysen must have a tab at Kelly's. He'd get the bill, Lindsey expected, and in due course International Surety would see it.

The waitress retrieved the car keys from Van Huysen's pants pocket. Together she and Lindsey poured Van Huysen into the Jaguar. She said,

'Where can I drop you, sir, before I take poor William home?'

Lindsey checked his wristwatch. If he caught the first available train, he could get back to 58th Street at a reasonable hour. He didn't see any reason to spend the night in New Haven, so he asked her to take him to the railroad station.

In the front seat Van Huysen stirred a little. 'You'll receive my bill in the morning, my good man. My very good man. Say, you are satisfied with services rendered, Lindsey, are you not?'

'Very.'

'Well, if you're not, say, you might try Dr. Selvatica.'

'Who's that?'

'Colleague of mine. I think. Never could quite find out. Doesn't know beans about classics or ancient history, but she's really great on modern Italy. I guess she's a she. First name is Mora. Mora Selvatica . . . ' He hiccupped. 'Have a lovely trip back to the big city. Merry Xmas, Lindsey.'

They had reached the railroad station and the waitress pulled the Jaguar up to the curb. She said, 'I'm sorry about that. He just hasn't been the same since . . . Well, I'll get him home. I'll put him to bed and cook supper for his little one. It's going to be a slow night at Kelly's anyway, with the students all out of town.'

Lindsey climbed from the Jaguar. He hefted his laptop and thanked her, adding, 'Thank Professor Van Huysen for me, too.'

She waved and pulled away from the curb.

12

Lindsey paid his cab fare from Grand Central and walked the short distance to his temporary home. He kept his computer at his side, the way a Western gunfighter kept his shootin' iron at the ready. He checked his watch as he made his way through the frozen streets. It was a little after 11:00 p.m. Nine-something in Denver. He didn't think Richelieu would be at his desk. He could leave a voice-mail message, or send him an email via KNP, or wait for morning. Then he could call his mother and her new husband, or his friend Eric Coffman, or . . .

There was an ambulance in front of the building, and a police car with flashing roof-lights. What in the world?

A uniformed cop stood outside the lobby door. Beyond him, Lindsey could see a couple of white-coated paramedics, another uniformed officer, and several figures in civvies.

The cop nearest Lindsey said, 'Please, no rubbernecking, sir. Just move along.'

Lindsey said, 'Is that Detective Sokolov?'

'You know Detective Sokolov?'

'Yes. I live in this building. I — '

'You *live* here? Maybe you better step inside, buddy.' The uniformed cop swung the door open.

The lobby was brightly lit and bustling with activity. The uniformed cop was trying to look important. A couple of technicians were scouring the lobby, dusting for fingerprints, picking up paper clips and matchsticks and putting them in baggies.

The paramedics were working over a bloody figure lying beside the battered wooden desk that Lou Halter shared with the Bermudez brothers. Lindsey got a look at the figure on the floor. He was lying in a blood slick, his arms out-stretched. There was no question, he was one of the Bermudez brothers. Lindsey couldn't see his badge from here. He'd met both brothers by now. He knew they weren't twins, but they were close in age and similar in appearance; he didn't know them well enough to tell which one he was looking at. But a copy of *Civil Procedure of the State of New York, Revised* lay just beyond Bermudez's fingers, its pages soaked with his blood. Lindsey knew then that he was looking at Benjamino.

He felt a rough hand on his arm. 'Mr. Lindsey, what are you doing here?'

He whirled and locked eyes with Marcie Sokolov. Then he gasped for breath, still clutching his laptop computer in its black canvas carrying case. He felt light-headed. Marcie Sokolov took him by the elbow and guided him to the old swivel chair that the lobby guards used.

'Sit down. It's already been dusted.'

He collapsed into the chair and looked up at her gratefully.

'You never see a stiff before?' Sokolov asked.

Lindsey had, as many as a man his age typically did. For the most part they were cleaned up and neatly dressed and laid out for burial. But he'd seen fresh corpses as well. The freshest he'd ever seen was that of Nathan ben Zinowicz, who had pointed a revolver at Lindsey and announced his intention of killing him, then reversed both his decision and the barrel of the revolver and blown away his own face and the back of his own head. Lindsey still had nightmares about that.

'I've seen bodies,' he managed to tell Sokolov. Through his light-headedness he took in odd details of his surroundings. He realized that Marcie Sokolov was wearing thin surgical gloves. Everybody in the room was wearing them except Lindsey.

She said, 'You know this fellow?' She jerked a thumb toward the body on the terrazzo.

'I know him. Knew. He's was a security guard in the building.'

She nodded agreeably. 'Figured as much. Considering that he's wearing a security guard's uniform and all. I'm not a detective for nothing, you know. Who is he?'

'Uh, Benjamino Bermudez.'

Sokolov nodded. 'Funny coincidence. His nametag says Bermudez, too. How do you know him? And what are you doing here at this hour of the night?'

'I'm . . . Cletus Berry had a place here. I'm using it while I'm in New York.'

'At this hour?'

'I, ah, I've been staying here, too. Cletus had it set up so he could stay over once in a while. I'm using it as an apartment for a few days.'

She snorted. 'What I'm interested in is, how come Mr. Bermudez caught a couple of bullets tonight, minding his own business, sitting in the lobby studying away at his law book? You have any idea, Mr. Lindsey?'

Lindsey looked about him. 'I'm still trying to figure out what happened.'

Sokolov smiled. 'It's hard to be certain, but I'll tell you what I think happened. Somebody came a-knock-knock-knocking at the door over there. Mr. Bermudez was sitting here, looked up and recognized the person at the door. He let him in and the visitor popped him.'

'How do you know he knew him?' Lindsey frowned.

'Think about it. If the visitor had been

a stranger, Bermudez would have waved him away. Late evening, building closed, go away, come again another day. You got that?'

Lindsey got it.

'Suppose the visitor had persisted — rapping at the glass with a key, maybe pointing a weapon. What would Bermudez do then?'

'He had a gun of his own. He wore a holster.'

'That's right. And his weapon is still in it. What's he do?'

'I think he'd duck under his desk. Try to get away.'

'Or maybe he'd go over to the door and let the visitor in. If the visitor was pointing a big scary cannon at him, he would, don't you think?'

'Wouldn't he draw his own weapon to defend himself?'

'You mean, play Quick-draw McGraw? Not smart. But Mr. Bermudez did neither, see? Didn't dive for cover. Didn't slap leather. He was between the desk and the front door when he was shot. No blood anywhere else in the lobby. No sign of a struggle. But look at his law book. He had it with him when he went to the door. Why would he do that?'

Lindsey waited.

'If the visitor was somebody he knew, somebody he felt confident with, he'd put his finger at his place in the book, carry the book with him, open the door with one hand and then return to the desk. Except he never returned to the desk.'

Lindsey nodded. 'Why would somebody do that? Why kill Mino Bermudez?'

'You tell me, Mr. Amateur Sleuth.'

'I can't tell you. But one thing I learned from murders I've worked on is that coincidences are very, very unusual. It's true, they happen. But they make me nervous.' He made a mental note to thank Lt. Dorothy Yamura, Berkeley Police Department, for the use of her line.

Sokolov put her hands on her hips. 'Thanks for the philosophy. Next time I see Immanuel Kant I'll pass it along. Now tell me what the hell you meant by that crack.'

'Okay,' Lindsey snapped. 'What I meant was, Berry rented space in this building. A few days ago he was murdered. The cops don't seem to be doing much about the case, but a tow-head boy from Colorado turns up and starts digging into the case, and actually moves into Berry's little nest. And somebody gets into the building after hours and offs poor Mino Bermudez. I'll bet you dollars to donuts that whoever killed Bermudez rode up to the sixth floor and inspected Berry's nest. Which is now my nest, of course.'

Sokolov said, 'Let's take a look.' She signaled a uniformed policeman to join them and they climbed aboard the elevator.

13

As the elevator approached the sixth floor, Sokolov jabbed Lindsey. 'Okay, cowboy, who had keys to the nest?'

'I don't know. Zissler. Me. Were there keys on Berry's body?'

'Yep. They're evidence now.'

'That's all I know of,' Lindsey said. 'But the landlord must have one, too.'

They stood outside Lindsey's door. Sokolov put her ear to the wood panel, then shook her head. She motioned Lindsey and the uniform out of the way, set herself against the wall beside the door, and knocked. 'Police. Open up. Police!'

No response.

She gestured to Lindsey, a hand motion that said as clearly as words, *give me the keys.* With her other hand she drew the revolver from her holster.

She unlocked the door and pushed it open, then crouched and ducked into the room, weapon at the ready.

Nothing happened.

Lindsey heard her grunt as she hit the light switch. The room was flooded with light. Sokolov said, 'Come on, then.' She motioned Lindsey inside, signaling the uniform to stay in the hallway.

'Just stand there, Mr. Lindsey. Turn slowly. Tell me if anything looks different to you. We'll have some technicians in here to dust for prints, but you eyeball the scene right now and tell me if anything is missing or added or moved around.'

Lindsey did as she instructed. He realized that he still had his laptop in his hand, and laid it on the futon.

'There's nothing missing. Nothing moved.'

'Look in the closet. Look in the bathroom.'

'Nothing. Nothing touched.' He rubbed his forehead, standing over Berry's computer. He frowned. 'I wonder . . . '

'What?'

'If somebody was here — would he know about the Nyagic policy?'

'What the hell are you talking about?'

171

He explained the term, the oddity of finding the old policy file on Berry's hard disk, and the problem he'd had cracking the shell of protective software that surrounded it.

'And you'd printed this policy out?'

'Not yet. I copied the file into my laptop and took it with me.' He indicated the computer lying on the futon.

'Took it with you? Took it with you where?'

Lindsey hesitated. 'Yale, in New Haven.'

Sokolov frowned. 'I hope you'll tell me about that. But not now. Unless you think there's some connection with your visitor. If you had one.'

'I don't know. I think there might be.'

Sokolov pursed her lips. 'Okay. Spill. I want the Reader's Digest Condensed Books version.'

'I had a meeting with a professor up at Yale. I took the train up there. We had a long conversation about the missing chariot — '

'What chariot are we talking about?'

'It's really just a toy. But it's very old, very valuable. I had to talk to Professor

Van Huysen about it. I copied the Nuargic file onto my laptop so I could study it on the train.'

Sokolov nodded. 'So you think this file was the reason for the break-in? You think somebody did break in here, do you, and took it?'

Lindsey nodded. 'I'm sure of it. I want to try something. I want to boot up Berry's computer and take a look at something.'

'And what is that?'

'Just let me try it, okay?'

Sokolov let out a hissing breath. 'All right, hold on.' She leaned her head out the door. 'Officer, go downstairs and send up a print tech. I want this computer dusted before Mr. Lindsey plays a tune.'

★ ★ ★

The technician was fast and there were plenty of fingerprints on the keyboard, and a few more elsewhere on the computer. Sokolov told Lindsey that most of them would probably be his own, or

173

Cletus Berry's. But if the intruder had touched the machine, they might pick up a fresh print.

'You can use it now. And while you're at it, here, put on these gloves. Just to stay on the safe side.' She pulled an extra pair of white surgical gloves from her pocket and handed them to Lindsey.

He sat down at the computer. He couldn't resist holding his gloved hands up and wriggling his fingers just once, like Liberace. Then he called up the directory of Berry's case files.

He whirled around in the swivel chair and told Sokolov that the Nyagic file was missing. 'It's gone. Erased.'

Sokolov shook her head. 'I don't know if this is a crime scene or not. No sign of breaking in. If somebody got in here, he was either one hell of a Raffles or he had a key to the joint. I could sure use a cup of joe. Mr. Lindsey, do you have the makings? Could I prevail on you to nuke me a cupful?'

Lindsey smiled and spooned instant coffee into a couple of cups and nuked it for Sokolov and himself. He smiled at

Sokolov across the rim of his cup. 'Raffles?'

'Ronald Colman, 1930.'

'David Niven, 1940.'

'John Barrymore, 1917.'

Lindsey said, 'You win.'

Sokolov said, 'Jesus, Lindsey, I didn't even play my ace. House Peters, 1925.'

She was showing an astonishing human side. And, more important, maybe she was coming around to Lindsey's belief that Cletus Berry's murder — and those of Frankie Fulton and Benjamino Bermudez, and maybe even those of Millicent Martin and the long-dead Massimo di Verolini — were more than unconnected, random tragedies.

Sokolov put her cup carefully on the floor beside the desk. 'That's a whole lot better. Now, what's so special about this file, and how could the mysterious stranger know how to steal or destroy it?'

Lindsey gave Sokolov a summary of the Silver Chariot story.

'Damn!' She looked out the window, toward Central Park. 'Sounds like the Maltese Falcon to me. Who are we looking for? Casper Gutman? Wilmer the gunsel? If Cletus Berry is Miles Archer and you're Sam Spade, who the hell does that make me? Brigid O'Shaugnessy or Effie Perine?' She turned back and looked at Lindsey. 'Never mind, I'm just being silly. What happened to the Nyagic file, then?'

Lindsey felt an urge to reach for Marcie Sokolov's hand. He'd been alone too long, and suddenly he was bantering classic movie trivia with a woman. With, he realized, an attractive woman. 'Whoever was here wiped the file from Berry's hard disk,' he said. 'If he's as computer-savvy as he seems to be, he downloaded the file first and carried it away on a floppy. I can log onto International Surety's master databank and find out whether he knew enough to erase it there, too. I don't know if there's a backup anywhere in IS, but it doesn't matter because I've got the file in my laptop.' He tilted his head toward the black canvas bag on the futon.

'Could you make a copy for me?' Sokolov asked.

'A breeze. I can copy it back onto Berry's machine and back into the big database. This is the second time it's been deleted and I've had to put it back. I'm sorry I can't print it out for you, because the printer isn't working. But I'll download it onto a floppy and you can have that.' He stopped. 'There is a confidentiality problem.'

'Mr. Lindsey, I can get a court order. Don't make me.'

He downloaded the file and handed it to Sokolov. She slipped it into her pocket.

They rode down in the elevator. In the creaking, swaying car, Sokolov suggested that Lindsey move to a hotel. 'Look here, whoever killed that guard in the lobby and got into your little fortress of solitude up there — '

'I was wondering about that,' Lindsey said. 'If he had a key, he was probably up there before. Wouldn't the guard know him? Wouldn't Benjamino just say, 'Hello there, Mr. Smith, cold enough for you tonight?' We already know that Mino knew the visitor. That whole business with the textbook. So why did the visitor kill him?'

Sokolov frowned. 'Okay, Mr. Amateur, you tell me.'

'Because,' Lindsey said, 'if Benjamino Bermudez knew that the visitor was up there so soon after Berry's death, he'd see a connection. The visitor would figure that Bermudez was smart enough to put two and two together and blow the whistle. No way the visitor was going to leave a witness to his visiting Berry's nest late at night, so soon after Berry's death. But he had to go there to delete the Nyagic file. He didn't know that I'd already found that file. And he certainly couldn't know that I'd have an old acquaintance who happened to be a software genius and could help me crack the lock on it. And he didn't know that I had a copy of the file in my laptop.'

'So the visitor thinks he's covered his trail now.'

'I think so.'

'I don't know.' Sokolov sounded worried. 'You could be next.'

'I'll be careful. I don't think he'll come

back here. And I'm sure the building will tighten up their security. And I suppose I should have the lock changed on my door. I'll have International Surety pay for that.'

The elevator door rolled back. In the terrazzo-floored lobby, the technicians had removed Benjamino Bermudez's body and cleaned up the pool of blood in which it had lain.

A harried-looking man in a badly outmoded brown suit was fidgeting nervously. When he caught sight of Marcie Sokolov's gold detective's badge, he introduced himself as the building manager. Lindsey had never seen him before.

A uniformed cop approached Sokolov and said that the building had been checked out. The manager had provided keys to the offices. There was no sign of an intruder hiding anywhere.

Sokolov and Lindsey traded glances. If the building manager had a key to every door in the building, the gates were wide open.

Sokolov said to Lindsey, 'I think we've

done all we can do tonight. If you want, you can come down to the shop tomorrow and we'll work on this some more.'

The building manager said, 'What am I going to do for a guard? Benjy was a good man.'

'Who comes on in the morning, Benjamino's brother or Lou Halter?' Lindsey asked him.

The manager furrowed his brow. His thin hair was disarrayed. 'I'd better call Rodrigo anyway. But Lou Halter's due. I guess I could call him now and start him early. Damn, that's going to put him into overtime.' He tilted his head and peered at Lindsey. 'How do you know my guards?'

'I was a friend of Cletus Berry's. I work for International Surety. I guess I'm your new tenant.'

The building manager studied Lindsey for a few seconds, nodded, and reached into his pocket for a cell phone. He punched in a pre-coded number. After half a minute he said, 'Rodrigo? Listen, Rodrigo, there's some bad news here for you.' He wandered to the rear of the lobby, crouched even lower into himself, and dropped his voice so Lindsey could no longer hear him.

By the time Lindsey rode upstairs again, he was exhausted. It had been a long day and it had ended in blood and death. He undressed and climbed into heavy pajamas, then brushed his teeth and washed his mouth out and climbed onto the futon. He put down his head and closed his eyes, then opened them again.

Something was blinking at him. It was the light on the answering machine.

For a moment he lay there watching the red light wink on and off. The call must have come in while he and Sokolov were in the lobby the second time. He crawled off the futon and hit the playback button.

'Thought I'd find you at home, chum. You want to chat some more, meet me at the Bird & Trane on Perry in the Village. I'll be there tomorrow night. Don't look for me, I'll look for you.'

The voice paused. Lindsey could hear

some noise in the background. It was a piercing screech, almost an inhuman scream.

'Gotta make my train,' the voice resumed. 'Tomorrow. Tennish.' The message ended with a click. The voice had been that of Victor Hopkins.

14

The telephone was ringing and Lindsey woke up, momentarily lost. The morning light was filtering through the window that looked northward across 58th Street. He was in New York, in Cletus Berry's live/work space, and the telephone was ringing. He crawled off the futon and picked up the handset.

'Mr. Lindsey, this is Petrus Berry phoning. We've never met, but maybe you saw me at the funeral home or at the cemetery.'

'I saw you, yes.'

'My brother spoke very well of you. He told me about rooming with you in Denver, and about a case he helped with. Something up in the Bronx.'

'Cletus was a fine man,' Lindsey said. 'I wish I'd known him better. I'm very sorry for what happened.'

There was a pause. 'Mr. Lindsey, Ester tells me that you're not satisfied with the police work on this case.'

'That's true. *Was* true. I've talked again with Detective Sokolov and I think she's taking it more seriously now. I think she may do some good work.'

'Then you think the NYPD is going to right this outrage?'

Lindsey drew a deep breath. 'No, sir. I think they're trying harder than they were. Detective Sokolov is. But frankly I'm not at all confident about it. I intend to keep working on the case.'

'I think I know a little bit about you, sir. From Cletus. You have a way of getting your teeth into a case and not letting go. You shake and shake and shake until something comes loose.'

'Well.' Lindsey didn't know what to say.

'I didn't say it to flatter you, Mr. Lindsey. Look here, I'm a retired police officer myself. I was ten years older than Cletus. I grew up in Pinopolis, South Carolina. It isn't much of a town, but my parents saw to it that I got a pretty good education. I was in the army for a while, then I went to college, and by then things had started changing in the south. I got a job on the local police force, put in my years, and now I've got my pension.'

He paused, then resumed. 'My brother, though, he came along later. He went off to see the world. Studied art history. Got himself a good job; earned his way to warrant officer in the army.'

'Ester told me that,' Lindsey said.

'Well, then after Cletus finished his military service, why, he'd seen Paris and Athens and Rome. There was nothing for him in Pinopolis. Especially not with an Italian wife. A white Italian wife, if you understand. He never brought her to Pinopolis. That was wise, I think. They just settled down up here in New York, and I guess they would have lived happily ever after if it hadn't been for — well, the perpetrator.'

Lindsey checked the time. It was a little before nine o'clock. 'Mr. Berry, let's work together on this.'

'That's what I wanted to ask you to do.'

'So when can we get together? And where?'

Petrus Berry told Lindsey that Zaffira Fornari had given him the use of her apartment guest room while he was in town. It was near her sister's home on 73rd Street. Zaffira had moved in with Ester and Anna Maria for the time being anyway, and the smaller apartment would have stood empty if Cletus didn't use it.

Lindsey said, 'Even so, why don't we meet at Ester's. She has a right to know what we're doing. And she may have some information we can use.'

'Later,' Berry said. 'I think we should talk first, Mr. Lindsey, just you and me, before we go up there.'

Lindsey agreed. Berry suggested that they meet at a restaurant on Second Avenue, just around the corner from Ester's apartment. They would have lunch, talk, and then head up to Ester's.

But before Lindsey got out of his nest, Marcie Sokolov phoned. 'You'd better get over to Midtown North.'

Lindsey hadn't phoned in to Ducky Richelieu's office in Denver yet. He asked, 'Is it urgent, Detective?'

'It's urgent.'

Richelieu would have to wait. But still, before he got moving he placed a brief

call to Manhattan East. He arranged to
have the lock changed on his temporary
digs, and to get a couple of toner
cartridges for the printer.

On his way out of the building, he
noticed a new lobby guard. He stopped
and introduced himself. The guard's
name was Hassan Muhammad. Lindsey
explained that he sometimes worked very
late hours. Hassan Muhammad said, 'I
am only here the few hours.'

'Yes, fine. Well, if you see me again,
you'll know me.' He scribbled Cletus
Berry's suite number on an International
Surety business card and handed it to
Hassan Muhammad. 'There may be some
other people around from my company.'

★   ★   ★

Detective Sokolov said, 'Sit down, Lindsey. I'm glad to see you here.'

'Why wouldn't I be here? You asked me
to come in.'

'Right. You want a cup of coffee?'

'Sure.'

She filled a heavy mug for him. It had a

Vassar College crest on the side, in gold. She was already drinking from a matching mug.

'You remember I told you we had an eye witness to the Fulton/Berry murders, Lindsey? And that we ID'd the shooter?'

'I remember. Johnny Thieu Ng.'

'The good news is, we found him. The bad news is, he's dead.'

Lindsey put his mug down on her desk with a thump.

'The worse news is, the source who ID'd him for us was with him. I don't suppose there's any harm in telling you his name now. Not that it would mean a lot. Bilbo Sax.' She raised an eyebrow. 'Ring a bell?'

Lindsey shook his head.

'Apparently Bilbo died at home. He lived on Amsterdam Avenue. Little basement apartment, pretty minimal, bare pipes on the ceiling, bare light bulbs, that kind of place. He lived alone there, just ol' Bilbo and a few rats. Neighborhood kids were playing spy. Too young to earn money as lookouts for the local drug dealers, they were pretending. Good training; when they get a little older they'll be experienced. Nice, hey?'

Lindsey waited.

'Well, they saw these two figures in the room. Not too much light there, and the windows were pretty grimy, of course, so the kids couldn't be certain. But they thought they saw the two of them, Johnny Thieu Ng and Bilbo Sax, naked. Kids actually managed to find a grownup who'd listen to them. Somebody's mom, most likely. She came and took a look and went home and phoned 911. Didn't leave her name, of course.'

Lindsey was trying to catch up. 'Just sitting around naked? So what?'

'They weren't sitting around. They were hanging. Both of them had leather belts around their necks, and they were hanging from the water pipes.'

Lindsey's hands went cold. He laced his fingers around the Vassar College mug, drawing the warmth of the porcelain into his hands. 'Suicide? Murder?'

'I think it was meant to look like accidental suicide. There were skin books strewn around. Lots of naked bodies, lots of people doing interesting things to themselves and each other.'

'I don't see the connection.'

'Of course not. Out there in God's country, the only sex you have is missionary position, right?'

Lindsey reddened. 'Not quite.'

'Well, it's supposed to get you off better. You buckle a belt around your neck so your breathing is cut off and then you — I'm sorry, Mr. Lindsey, am I upsetting you?'

Lindsey shook his head.

'It's supposed to be the maximum male orgasm. I wouldn't know about that.' She took a sip of coffee. 'Dangerous to play around with if you don't have somebody there to make sure you don't suffocate. And Johnny and Bilbo — I think we were supposed to figure that they were playing together with their skin books and they both got carried away. They were going to try it together, and it didn't work. Or it worked too well, depending on how you look at it.'

She set her coffee mug on her desk and leaned forward on her elbows. 'Do you buy it, Mr. Lindsey? No? Neither do I. And there's something else I didn't tell you. Johnny and Bilbo had both been beaten before they were hanged. There were fresh bruises on their faces and arms. As if they'd been trying to defend themselves.' She dropped her hands into her lap. 'We'll see what the coroner has to say, but right now it looks as if they were beaten unconscious, then strangled and strung up so it would look like a double sex-strangulation.'

Lindsey shook his head. 'Who do you think did it? And why?'

'Good questions. I wish I had the answers. But I'll tell you this — the more bodies that turn up, and the more strands we can tie between them, the more certain I am that we'll find a nice spider web with some fat son-of-a-bitch spider sitting in the middle of it. Sooner or later, that web is going to come together. And when it does, we'll have our killer.'

'Who's dead so far?'

Together, they made the list, in order of death.

Millicent Martin.
Frankie Fulton.
Cletus Berry.
Benjamino Bermudez.
Johnny Thieu Ng.
Bilbo Sax.

Detective Sokolov said, 'Have we left anyone out?'

'Massimo di Verolini.'

'Who in hell is that?'

Lindsey told her about the *Fior di Rimini* and the body found in the crate that should have contained the Silver Chariot when that ship unloaded in Italy in 1940.

'Do you really think there's a connection, Lindsey? Do you mind if I drop the 'mister'? And you can call me Sokolov. Only my closest friends have that privilege. Do you really think this di Verolini who's been dead for almost sixty years is connected to the others?'

'Sokolov. Sure.' Lindsey studied the wall clock behind the detective. He had plenty of time to meet Petrus Berry. 'It's going to take two more names to make that web of yours appear, Sokolov, but I think it's going to happen, and I think di Verolini is going to be part of it.'

Sokolov arched an eyebrow. 'Two more corpses? We've got six corpses already. Seven, if you count what's-his-name, Massimo di Verolini.'

'Two more names,' Lindsey corrected. 'Not necessarily dead ones. Randolph Amoroso and Alcide Castellini.'

'Holy cow! What are you talking about?' Sokolov reached across her desk and grasped the curved edge nearest to him. 'Do you know what the hell you're talking about?'

'Listen.' Lindsey lowered his voice. 'The first I knew about this was when I heard that my friend had been murdered. Then I found out he'd been murdered with Frankie Fulton. Then the *Daily News* published a file photo of Fulton together with Alcide Castellini and a showgirl named Millicent Martin. She'd also been murdered in a nasty, sexually suggestive way.'

'Go on.'

'I saw Castellini buddying it up with

Congressman Amoroso at his rally in Times Square the other day. And I picked up an Amoroso-for-Senate brochure, and there he is using the Silver Chariot as a campaign logo.'

Sokolov frowned. 'I've seen it.'

'Okay. The Silver Chariot — the real Silver Chariot — was on display in the Italian pavilion at the 1939 World's Fair. When it was shipped back to Italy in 1940, it mysteriously disappeared and Massimo di Verolini's corpse turned up in its place.'

Sokolov was scowling but Lindsey kept on going.

'Somebody breaks into Cletus Berry's pad in the Torrington Tower and wipes the Nyagic file from his computer. That's the file on the chariot, you see? Wipes it, and maybe swipes it. And deletes the file from the International Surety databank, not knowing that I've got a copy.'

Sokolov nodded grimly.

'And,' Lindsey wound up, 'Bilbo Sax rats on Johnny Thieu Ng for the Hell's Kitchen killings, and Bilbo and Johnny die together in a faked accidental suicide that you yourself tell me was really another double murder. So what do you think?'

'You've tried to pull all these killings together, but I don't see a motive,' Sokolov answered. 'I don't see what they mean. You gotta show me a motive.'

'The chariot.'

'What about the chariot?'

'That's what I was doing in New Haven yesterday — talking with this classics professor at Yale. William Van Huysen. He even wrote part of Amoroso's brochure, the part about the chariot. I'm trying to get a line on that chariot.'

'And?'

'And it's a symbol of Roman power. One of those legends, you know, like the Holy Grail or a fragment of the True Cross. *Down through the centuries* . . . That kind of thing. Randolph Amoroso is running his campaign on *America the New Rome*, right? Every politician who's owned the chariot goes on to greatness. Maybe even King Solomon — if you believe Van Huysen. Alexander the Great. Julius Caesar. Charlemagne. Mussolini. When each of them lost the chariot, he lost his empire, or he died young, or the thing came apart on him. The chariot vanished in 1940, and it was all downhill for Mussolini after that. And the chariot has never resurfaced.'

'Do you have any idea where the chariot is now, Lindsey?'

'I don't. But I think Cletus Berry did. And I think Alcide Castellini — *eminence grisé* of New York antique dealers, or so I've been told — '

'That's putting it very kindly.'

'I think Alcide Castellini is after the chariot, doing acquisition work for Randolph Amoroso. I figure we can follow Castellini, and if he finds the chariot, the whole thing will fall into place. Including the murders. Or better yet, if we can beat Castellini to the chariot, he'll come to us.'

15

Lindsey warmed up on a cross-town bus ride, then froze walking up Second Avenue looking for the restaurant Petrus Berry had suggested. He stopped at a candy store and picked up a copy of the *Post*. There was nothing on the murders of Johnny Thieu Ng and Bilbo Sax. They must be too ordinary for New York. Or maybe nobody had got any good photos of the corpses dangling from the water pipes, and without the pictures, the editor had decided that nobody would bother to read the story.

After another half-block Lindsey spotted the restaurant. It was a dark, cavernous place with a wooden sign outside announcing its name as the Bear Garden. The temperature outside was close to zero; inside the Bear Garden, a massive log blazed in a stone fireplace.

Lindsey recognized Petrus Berry almost at once. He was settled at a wooden table.

Anna Maria Berry sat opposite him. A bowl of chili stood in front of each of them. Petrus Berry sat quietly watching over the girl, sipping a glass of red wine.

Lindsey crossed the room. It was late for lunch, and the place was nearly empty.

Petrus Berry stood up and shook hands with Lindsey. 'You know my niece, Anna Maria?'

Lindsey nodded. He took an empty chair.

'Mr. Lindsey, Ester and Zaffira tell me that you've been doing a lot of work. I wish you'd tell me what you know. Are you getting anywhere?'

Before Lindsey could answer, a waiter appeared and asked what he'd like. He looked at the chili and nodded. 'One of those, please. And a cappuccino.' Then he addressed the child. 'Is this going to upset you, Anna Maria?'

She laid her spoon on the table and looked at Lindsey. The look in her eyes was not the look of a ten-year-old. 'I want to know who killed my dad. I want him caught and punished. You go ahead.'

Lindsey repeated the facts and the

partial theory he'd worked out with Marcie Sokolov. He held his hands up and ticked of the list of murders on his fingers. When he finished, he didn't wait for Petrus Berry to comment or to ask him any further questions. Instead he said, 'There's a connection, and I think it's the chariot. What I need to know is what Cletus was doing in Italy back in the '70s.'

'That's when he met Ester,' Petrus supplied.

'I know that. What was he doing for the army? He was part of NATO, right?'

Petrus nodded.

'What were his duties? And what were his off-duty connections? Could he have had something to do with the chariot?'

'I'm ten years older, Lindsey. I was in the army, too, but I was in and back out again before Cletus ever put on khaki. I was military police. I guess that was how I got into cop work when I got back home — from playing traffic cop on an army base. I'm afraid I don't know anything about Italy.'

'I do,' Anna said.

Lindsey tilted his head. 'What do you know? What you study in school?'

The question elicited a rare smile from the child. 'We don't learn much about Italy at Beth Israel.' She looked up at Lindsey.

What eyes! Dark Italian eyes. Dark Hebrew, dark African eyes.

'But I want to learn about my heritage. I have a rich heritage.'

She was the future, Lindsey thought.

'I want to learn about my Jewish and Italian and African roots. I talk about it with my cousin all the time. Mosé Lazarini.'

'Your cousin.' Lindsey's food had arrived, and his cappuccino. He spread a linen napkin on his lap.

'My cousin Mosé lives in Rome. He's my first cousin on my mother's side. I met him in a history chat group. It was great, finding a cousin I didn't even know about.'

'What kind of chat group? Were you in Italy?'

'A computer chat group on the net. I was looking for something about Italian

Jews. There's nothing in my school books. My mom says we were in Italy for thousands of years.'

'I know. She told me. I didn't know that.'

'We were in Rome before the Christians were. Before there were any Christians. My mom told me about it, but I wanted to know some more. So I was just surfing around, looking in on discussion groups, and here was somebody talking about Jews in Italy. I introduced myself, and we went off to a private room — '

'Wait a minute. Private room?'

'When you're in a group on the net, you can set up a private room and talk to each other.'

'Like email.'

'A lot like email. Only in real time. Like chatting. But it's in private.'

'Tell me,' Lindsey said, 'what have you learned from your cousin?' She started to answer, but he added, 'Something I forgot. I went up to New Haven yesterday and talked to a Professor Van Huysen. He — '

'I know William.' Anna grinned.

'You've been to Yale?'

'No, he's in our chat group. He's a little stodgy but he is fairly knowledgeable.'

Fairly knowledgeable. Lindsey restrained a laugh 'That's funny,' he managed, 'he didn't mention you.'

Anna grinned. 'Maybe he did.' She looked at Petrus. 'Uncle Peter, should I tell him? It's a secret, Mosé's and my secret.'

'You told me, darling. Mr. Lindsey is here to help us.' He turned to Lindsey. 'Would you make a confidential disclosure pledge?'

Lindsey agreed.

'My cousin and I, once we got to know each other, we made up another screen persona.'

'Screen persona.' Lindsey waited. Petrus grinned, proud of his brother's child.

'A made-up identity. You know, I learned about them when I was in a flirt group.'

'A flirt group.' Lindsey was floundering.

'You know, it's a chat group where kids go to flirt. I thought it was pretty exciting at first. Boys would ask you to describe yourself, and how old are you, and did you ever — well ... ' She blushed. 'Anyway, the way some of them described themselves sounded kind of fishy. Then I talked to my friend Shoshana. She's older than I am, seven months and eleven days. She told me that kids make up screen personas and just make up stories and flirt. She told me that sometimes adults sneak into flirt groups. Some of them are real scumbags. There was one man in Ohio, he pretended he was a teenager and he made a date with a girl he met in a flirt group. I knew her from the group; she lives in Cleveland. He came to pick her up at her house and the girl's father shot him. He deserved it.'

Lindsey said gently, 'You were telling me about Professor Van Huysen.'

'Oh, yeah. Uncle Pete, could I have a cocoa? I love cocoa in winter.'

Petrus signaled to the waiter.

'See, the history group isn't just kids. Sometimes people talk about who they are. There are teachers and professors. There's one woman who wrote a book about pre-Columbian civilizations in Chile and Colombia. And a lot of college students and high school students. I think Mosé and I are the youngest members. Nobody knows how young we are. Mosé is my age. He wants to visit me. He thinks it's cool that I'm half-African. He thinks it's cool being Italian and Jewish, but he's never seen an Italian-African-American Jew. I sent him my picture by snail-mail and he sent me his, but he wants to meet me someday. If I had a scanner I could have zapped my picture, but I don't have one yet.'

Anna's cocoa arrived in a huge mug. She sipped it and continued. 'Mosé and I made up a persona, a history professor who travels back and forth between America and Italy. Her name is Mora Selvatica.'

Lindsey dropped his spoon. 'You are Mora Selvatica?'

'Did William say we were friends?'

'Uh — not exactly. He was, well, pretty drunk.'

'I know he drinks. We've had some chats in chat rooms. William is divorced and he has a little boy, and he asks Dr. Selvatica for advice. We tell him we need to think about it and we ask our parents, Mosé and I do.' She stopped and grabbed her napkin and rubbed her eyes.

'I'm sorry, Anna Maria,' Lindsey said. 'Maybe we should stop. Do you want to go home? Do you think your mother is home yet?'

Petrus Berry shook his head. 'Ester went to the lawyer's. Zaffira's with her. Anna Maria and I are spending the day together.' He pulled an oversized bandanna from his pocket and held it to Anna Maria's nose until she blew her nose into it. She put her mouth to his ear and he nodded assent. She jumped from his lap and headed deeper into the Bear Garden.

'Pit stop,' Petrus said. 'Through it all, when nature calls, we answer.'

'Do you have a family of your own?' Lindsey asked.

'No. Never met the right woman. Always thought I'd get married. Always thought the next woman I met would be the right one. I had plenty of time. Woke up one morning and looked in the mirror and my hair was gray, and I went to work and they were throwing a retirement party for me.' He nodded in the direction Anna had taken. 'I never thought a little Italian Jewish girl would be the only thing I care about in this world, but she is.'

'I understand.'

Petrus leaned across the table. 'Listen, you're staying in Cletus's pad. I'd get out of there if I were you.'

'I got that same suggestion from Marcie Sokolov. But look, whoever was up there and deleted the Nyagic file doesn't know that I broke the lock and copied the file. He thinks he's safe. It'd be more suspicious if I moved out than if I stayed, don't you see?'

Petrus frowned. 'What Nyagic file?'

Lindsey explained.

'I see. But I still don't think you're safe there. Did Sokolov offer to put you in a police safe-house?'

'We didn't get that far.'

'Well then — tell you what. Zaffira has

her own place. She's given it to me while I'm in town, and she's staying with Ester. Better for Ester to have her sister with her. Better for Anna Maria too, probably.' He paused. 'If you don't want to move into a hotel, you could move in with me. Into Zaffira's place.'

Lindsey considered. He didn't need access to Cletus Berry's paper files; everything was in International Surety's databank, and he could get at anything he needed through KlameNet/Plus. Besides, the key item was the Nyagic file, and that was in his laptop.

He spotted Anna returning from the ladies' room. 'Okay, Petrus. I think you're right.'

He found a pay phone and located Moe Zissler at Manhattan East. He told Zissler he was moving out of Cletus Berry's nest and would come by for his belongings. Zissler was to remove Berry's computer and all other IS property and return them to Manhattan East, and pack up Berry's clothing and personal effects and wait for word from Berry's widow about their disposal.

Petrus patted Anna on the shoulder. 'Mr. Lindsey's going to stay at Aunt Zaffira's with me. We're going to move his things now. You want to come along with us?'

She agreed. They took a cab to 58th and Seventh.

Lou Halter was on duty in the lobby. He looked up as Lindsey entered along with Anna and her uncle. He gasped and reached toward his holster, then stopped and held his hand out. It was trembling. His face was ashen. To Lindsey he suddenly looked more like eighty than sixty-five.

'He gave me a start,' Halter said, jerking his head toward Petrus Berry. 'He looks like Mr. Berry. You know about Mino Bermudez? I'm getting out of here. I'm turning in my gun. I don't want any part of this. I didn't want a gun to start with, but the agency pays a bonus if you'll carry a gun. But I don't want this job anymore anyhow. I'll take my social security and sit in my little house and do the crossword puzzles. I don't ask much and I don't need much and I don't need this, I'll tell you that for sure.'

As they walked to the elevator, Lindsey said, 'He's Mr. Berry's brother.'

When they entered the rooms upstairs, Anna said, 'Daddy brought me here. He showed me his other office; it was on Lexington and 53rd. I wasn't supposed to let on that I knew about his other office.'

Lindsey packed his belongings while he listened.

'Once Daddy brought me up here to help him with his computer. He wasn't really very good at it. He had this old insurance file on his disk. He told me he downloaded it from the company database, and he couldn't open it. I took a look at it and figured it out. It was easy. I showed him how to do it, and he said that he'd just keep the lock on it except when he wanted to use the file.'

So much for security, Lindsey thought.

Downstairs they caught another cab. Lindsey let the cabbie stow his flight bag in the trunk. He held on to his laptop.

★ ★ ★

Zaffira's apartment was a block north of Ester's, on 74th Street east of Second Avenue. The building was an old brownstone. Zaffira's apartment was on the third story, in the rear. Anna helped her uncle heft Lindsey's flight bag up the stairs. Petrus had insisted on carrying the bag, and Lindsey had toted his laptop.

Petrus Berry's key opened both the street door and the front door of the apartment. He followed Lindsey and Anna inside. 'Have to get another key for you,' he grunted.

Lindsey asked where the telephone was and Petrus pointed it out. 'I need to check in with my boss,' he said. 'International Surety will pay.'

'Come on,' Petrus said to Anna, 'let's give Mr. Lindsey some privacy.' To Lindsey he said, 'We'll go and browse that candy store down near the Bear Garden.'

'Sure, they always have good comic books and computer magazines,' Anna said.

Lindsey punched in Desmond Richelieu's private number. When Richelieu answered, Lindsey brought him up to date on the case.

Richelieu listened until Lindsey finished. Then he said, 'I've been checking with Legal. You know we paid out that old claim back in forty-something.'

'I know it.'

'You think this chariot really exists, Lindsey? Did it ever, or is it just a myth? And does it exist now?'

Lindsey told him that he was pretty sure that the chariot was real, that it was very old, and that it had actually existed as recently as 1940.

Richelieu snapped, 'I wouldn't call 1940 very recent.'

Lindsey didn't rise to the bait. 'Whatever. That was the last time we're pretty sure it was around. It was in New York. It was supposed to be aboard the *Fior di Rimini*. It wasn't in the packing case when it was opened in La Spezia.'

It was the mysterious Salvatore Castellini who had both discovered the loss of the chariot and the body of Massimo di Verolini. And it was Alcide Castellini who seemed to lurk behind every brutal event in Lindsey's investigation.

'Let me approach this from another angle,' Richelieu said. 'Let me ask you this. What do you think that chariot is worth, if it still exists, and if you could turn it up?'

'Van Huysen would know that better than I would. But it'd be priceless. I mean, it's an art treasure. It's a historical artifact. There's no way you can put a price on it.'

'Well, here's what Legal says, Lindsey. I think you've been hanging out with those artsy types too much lately. You're an insurance man, remember? International Surety forked out five million bucks to save some Italian lollapalooza's political ass fifty years ago. Five million at five percent compound interest for fifty years — I'm rounding, don't interrupt — is now worth on the order of $57,336,949.'

Lindsey gulped. 'Uh.'

'I want you to find out who killed Cletus Berry, Lindsey. I want to string the bastard up as high as I can reach. That's because I take care of my kiddies. I couldn't do less. J. Edgar would never let me do less. But you'd better hope that little chariot still exists, and you'd better find it. If you do, International Surety returns it to the grateful government of the Republic of Italy, along with a claim for the return of the five million we paid them back in Harry Truman's day. With interest.'

'Uh,' Lindsey said again.

'So get on it!' Richelieu hung up.

16

The Bird & Trane was dark, noisy and crowded. To Lindsey it looked as if every college student in the eastern half of the country had descended on the club, along with a healthy sprinkling of yuppies, a smattering of cyberpunks and a handful of revenants of the Jack Kerouac generation.

He'd paid a door charge and squeezed into the place. There was an ornate wooden bar. The long mirror behind it was decorated with Christmas wreaths, Santas and Rudolphs. The walls had been painted a flat black. Couples huddled over flickering candles in red jars on tiny round tables.

Lindsey looked around for Victor Hopkins. No sign of the young man. He managed to work his way up to the bar. There were no unoccupied stools. When the bartender condescended to notice him, he ordered a bottle of beer. Anything that came sealed was probably safest.

A woman to Lindsey's left turned and ran her eyes up and down him. She looked amused. 'You lose someone, granddad?' she asked.

'Matter of fact,' he said, 'I'm supposed to meet somebody here.'

The pallid female grinned. 'Good luck.' She snickered and leaned over her green drink, sipping through a short, opaque plastic straw.

Lindsey lifted his bottle — no, glass — and wiped the rim with his hand. He tasted the beer. At least it was cold. The club had been dark when he'd arrived, or so he'd thought, but now it grew darker. A crimson spotlight picked out a woman on the bandstand. She detached one of the microphones from its metallic stand and announced the band. Lindsey had never heard of them. They trooped onto the stage and began to play.

Someone had him by the elbow. He turned and saw Victor Hopkins. 'Do you have to be so damned melodramatic, Victor?'

Hopkins tugged him toward the entrance.

Outside the Bird & Trane, Perry Street was surprisingly busy. The population was a mixture of the well-dressed and the grungy. Taxis dropped off mixed and unmixed couples who disappeared into bars and apartment buildings.

Hopkins pulled Lindsey against a brick wall. He said, 'I've got some more information for you. About Millicent Martin and Alcide Castellini.'

'That I want to hear.'

Hopkins looked around like a character in a silly spy movie. Then Lindsey thought of two bodies in the ice in an alley in Hell's Kitchen, and of two more in a basement apartment in Harlem. Maybe Hopkins wasn't so silly.

Hopkins tugged at Lindsey's elbow again. 'I don't want to stay in one place too long.'

When they reached a corner, Hopkins tugged Lindsey around it. Lindsey looked up at the sign and read *West 4th Street*. There weren't as many commercial establishments here, and most of the residential windows were dark, but streetlights illuminated the sidewalks.

'You know that photo of Millie with Fulton and Castellini?'

Lindsey grunted agreement. 'Castellini keeps turning up,' he said. 'There are too many corpses in this tangle, and Castellini always seems to be around the edges.'

'Millie worked for him.'

'Doing what?'

'Castellini brought antiques into the US. Artworks and antiques. Some of them had questionable provenances. Know what I mean?'

Lindsey grunted assent.

'Customs had a line on Castellini. So he uses mules. He hires solid citizens — semi-solid, anyway. Go to France, go to Italy, go to an address and pick up a package and bring it back with you.'

'Uh-huh.' Lindsey frowned. 'But they still need to come through customs.'

'That's the whole point of using mules. Look, Millie comes through customs with a minor masterpiece and a bill of sale that says it's a *reproduction*, see, a *copy* worth fifty bucks or a hundred bucks. Castellini puts the whole thing together. He travels back and forth to Europe every couple of months making deals. But he never actually brings anything back with him except a little paperwork. Or ships anything back at all. They're too smart, they're onto him, they'd nail him in a second.'

A streetlight had burned out on West 4th Street. Something huddled against the stoop of a brownstone. Shifted. Probably some derelict who had settled down for the night, cheered by the layers of a sleeping bag and the contents of a bottle of wine. Lindsey and Hopkins gave the shadow a wide berth.

Hopkins continued, 'But some housewife from Omaha jets in from Europe and proudly declares a genuine reproduction of a panel by Cosmè Tura. She bought it in a shop in the Piazza Santa Maria for ninety US bucks and she has a receipt to prove it. She gets waved through customs, and a week later Alcide Castellini is supplying a *genuine* Tura panel to some Fifth Avenue collector. This dude knows the real from the phony, and what he buys is no phony. There's even a legitimate bill of sale. That's what Castellini carried home in his briefcase, while the mule was waving the phony bill of sale at the customs inspectors.'

The stoop of another brownstone loomed ahead of them, jutting onto the sidewalk. Something rose from the blackness beside it. A vaguely human shape raised its arm and pointed at Lindsey and Hopkins. Blond hair so pale it was almost luminous swung around the head. An errant ray of light glinted off metal. From behind them a voice shouted, *'G'down!'*

Lindsey felt Hopkins shove him to the sidewalk and crash on top of him. He heard two firearms discharge. A single shot came from behind him, from the direction of the Bird & Trane. A fusillade sounded from ahead of him, and sparks flew from buildings where stray shots struck. He felt Hopkins jerk once and heard him grunt with the impact of a bullet.

Someone ran toward Lindsey. He felt Hopkins lifted off him. Lindsey's own face was pressed into the frozen slush at the edge of the curb. Someone grabbed his shoulder and turned him over. He looked up and blinked at the worried face of Petrus Berry peering into his own.

Berry lowered him to the cold cement and trotted away along West 4th street. Lindsey struggled to his knees and looked at Victor Hopkins. Blood was bubbling from his mouth and gushing from a hole the size of a baseball in his throat.

There was no question about Victor Hopkins.

Lights were springing up in windows along the street. Lindsey ran in the direction Berry had run and picked up a trail of blood. He followed the trail, running a few yards, pulling up short of breath, then staggering on. He saw a broad-shouldered figure crouching ahead of him.

Petrus Berry clutched a revolver in one hand. He raised his eyes from the figure lying on the sidewalk and shook his head.

Lindsey panted, 'Hopkins is dead.'

Petrus said, 'So is this one.' He pointed at the figure on the sidewalk. The face showed no discernible gender or race. Its age was hard to judge. The body could belong to someone who had died after fifteen years of abuse or twice that many of a less damaging lifestyle. The flowing platinum hair was done in a long-out-of-style pageboy bob.

'You recognize this person?' Petrus asked.

'No. Not a clue.'

The body had a single hole in its chest. Petrus was either a sharpshooter or lucky.

Petus said, 'The police should be here any minute. Listen — you hear sirens?'

The whooping and wailing were coming closer. 'Maybe one of us should go back and stay with Hopkins,' Lindsey suggested. 'Show the cops the way when they get there.'

'Not a chance. I don't want us separated, and I don't want to leave this body unguarded. You can bet it'll get up and walk away if we don't keep watch.'

A police cruiser came wailing past, its roof-lights flashing. Petrus Berry waved at the car. He still had his revolver in his hand.

The cruiser screeched to a halt. A

uniformed cop jumped out, pointing a weapon at Berry and Lindsey. Without waiting for orders, Lindsey raised his hands in the air. Berry held his hands away from his body, slowly placed his revolver on the sidewalk and took two steps away from it.

The uniformed officer moved toward them. 'Get away from the gun and get down on the ground.'

They didn't argue. Berry was an old cop himself, and Lindsey had worked with police too often to do anything stupid. He tried to tell himself that it was okay; that everything would get sorted out. But Victor Hopkins was not okay, and neither was the strange being who had killed him.

Lindsey felt handcuffs snapped around his wrists, and heard another set go onto Berry. 'I'm sorry I got you into this mess, Petrus,' he said. 'I never thought anything like this would happen to us.'

'I followed you, Lindsey. You didn't drag me along.'

'Shut up,' the cop said. 'Can you sit up? Good. Get over to the wall there and sit

222

with your backs to it.'

When Berry and Lindsey had complied, the cop said, 'Jesus, Joseph and Mary. What the hell happened here? We got a call from somebody over by Waverly.'

Berry said, 'There's a body there.' He nodded toward the dead gun-slinger. 'This one did it. Used an Uzi or a Tek, I think. I killed him. That's my .38 on the ground.' He gestured again with his head.

The cop stood over them, looking down. 'You're pretty cool, mister, for a guy in in big trouble.'

Berry looked up at the cop and smiled. 'I'm a retired police officer. You'll find my ID and my concealed weapon permit in my wallet.'

The cop nodded. 'That's good.'

'The permit is from Pinopolis, South Carolina,' Berry added.

'That's bad,' the cop said.

17

It took a lot of persuasion to get them to call Marcie Sokolov. Once they did, it took her a while to arrive at the crime scene. Yellow ribbons were up, coroner's technicians and forensics squads were on site, and Lindsey and Petrus were out of their handcuffs but in a kind of informal custody.

The detective in charge of the scene was a Lieutenant MacArthur. He conferred briefly with Sokolov. They were out of earshot of Lindsey. After a little while MacArthur gestured to Petrus Berry and Berry joined the group.

Lindsey watched the tension dissipate among the three of them, to be replaced by the camaraderie of cops being cops together. MacArthur had already taken Lindsey's and Berry's stories. Lindsey saw a handshake exchanged between Sokolov and Berry. He could follow the bobbing heads and read the body language. Sokolov was offering her condolences to Petrus. She must have seen him at the cemetery, but then Sokolov had been an observer at the funeral; now she was a friend in need.

She crooked at finger at Lindsey. He joined the group. MacArthur said, 'Your story checks out, sir. You don't know what a lucky stiff you are. Chief Berry here — '

'Chief?' Lindsey exclaimed. 'You didn't tell me.'

'Pinopolis is just a small town,' Berry said.

'Chief Berry,' MacArthur went on, 'was worried about you, Mr. Lindsey. If he hadn't taken it upon himself to appoint himself bodyguard, you'd be back there with your friend on Waverly Place.' He had a pad and a pen in his hand, and used the pen to indicate Marcie Sokolov. 'Detective Sokolov is going to handle this matter. I'm just as happy; I've got plenty of scrapple on my plate already. I'm just going to make sure that the boys and girls do their job right. Once the scene is cleared I'll do my paperwork, and then I'll be delighted to place things in your capable hands, Detective Sokolov. May you catch all the bad guys and never miss a clue.' He made a mock-military salute. 'Lady and gentleman, I leave you to your affairs.'

'Thanks, Lieutenant, sir,' Sokolov said. She looked from Lindsey to Berry. 'I wish you'd checked in with me sooner, Chief.'

'Sorry,' Berry said. 'I didn't really expect to get so involved. Thought I'd pay a courtesy call and then head home. But I'm here for the duration now.'

'Glad to have you.' She blew a long plume of white breath from her mouth.

'I want to walk down and have a look at the bodies,' Sokolov said. 'Chief, you'd better recover your weapon there or it'll end up in a pawnshop. Good. Now, MacArthur knew the shooter, and he tells me that you knew the fellow with the beard, Lindsey. Is that true?'

'His name was Victor Hopkins.' Lindsey filled her in on his connection with Hopkins, about Hopkins's connection with Millicent Martin, and Hopkins's theory about her being a mule for Alcide Castellini.

Sokolov nodded. 'That's no surprise about Castellini.'

'Then why haven't you gone after him?' Lindsey demanded. 'Everywhere I turn, I come up against Alcide Castellini. Why don't you get on his case?'

Sokolov smiled bitterly. 'We are on his case. Have been for months. You know what happens when we go after some thug with deep pockets. First of all, Castellini is smart enough to cover his tracks, so we haven't been able to build a case against him for anything substantial.' She took a deep breath. 'And if we ever did put him in a courtroom, what do you think would happen? He'd bring in a squad of overpriced mouthpieces and tie us up for a million years.'

'You get one once in a while. Didn't you finally get John Gotti?'

Her brittle smile softened a little. 'Once in a while, that's right. It does give me hope.' She swung her arms vigorously, hugging herself. 'Come on, boys, let's go look at the stiffs.'

She walked them past the yellow tape and they bent to peer at the mortal remains of the shooter. The body lay in the middle of a chalked outline, and an inverted V-shaped piece of cardboard with a number on it had been placed on the dead shooter's chest alongside the hole where Berry's .38 slug had entered.

Sokolov looked at Berry. 'You did this, Chief? First shot?'

'Got a lot of practice in the army. Figured I ought to keep up my skills once I got on the force.'

Sokolov whistled. 'Either of you gentlemen recognize this other cadaver?'

The platinum hair still framed the dead face. Lindsey bent, then straightened. 'No idea in the world.'

'Chief?'

'Total stranger. I don't keep up too well with wanted posters, though.'

Sokolov snorted. 'You wouldn't have seen one on this fella. Merle Oates. Male caucasian, age 20. I guess you caught him out of season. His favorite trick is to dress up like a whore when he's on a hit. You'd be surprised how often it works. I guess it's too cold for that tonight, but he's got his favorite wig on, anyway.' She leaned over the body. 'Bye-bye, Merle.' Then she straightened and called an evidence technician who was working nearby. 'Hey, fella. Where's his piece?'

The technician looked at her. 'I didn't see any piece.'

'All right.' Sokolov sighed. 'Chief Berry, you say he was using a streetsweeper?'

'I didn't get a clear look at his piece, but it sure sounded like one. And those muzzle-flashes had to come from an automatic. Nobody's finger is that fast.'

'They found some casings and a couple of slugs. I'm sure you're right. We'll keep looking for the piece. What chance it went down a sewer grating? It's amazing how often they do that . . . Okay, let's take a peep at the other cadaver.'

They ducked under another strand of yellow tape to reach it.

'What do you think, Lindsey? Was Merle after you or was he after Victor here? What's your professional amateur judgment?'

Lindsey was perplexed. 'Hopkins has been in hiding. I thought he was acting paranoid about meeting me, sending messages through the *Times* — '

'What about the *Times*?' Sokolov asked sharply.

Lindsey explained about Amy Baines and about Hopkins's unwillingness to give Lindsey his address or phone number.

'Huh!' Sokolov turned her face upward, as if she might find a message written on the moon. Maybe the Bat Signal. 'Here's what I'm gonna do,' she said. 'I'm gonna bend the rules a little. Chief Berry, when one of our officers discharges a firearm in public, we have to take away his piece and put him on desk duty or administrative leave until there's a hearing on the incident.'

'You want my piece, Detective?'

'Please.'

He placed his revolver on her palm. She slipped it into a pocket of her heavy winter coat. 'Thanks,' she said, then walked over to a group of uniforms and dragged one of them back with her. She got the officer's name. 'Okay, Officer Gulbenkian, I'm Detective Sokolov. You know me, right?'

'Yes, ma'am.'

'Good. Meet Chief Berry and Mr. Lindsey.'

Officer Gulbenkian nodded twice.

'Here we go,' Sokolov said. 'I'm convening a special emergency hearing into the shootings of Victor Hopkins and Merle Oates, with particular attention to the conduct of Retired Chief of Police Petrus Berry, Pinopolis, South Carolina PD. You got that, officer?'

'You want me to take notes, Detective Sokolov?' Gulbenkian asked.

'Please.'

He opened a notebook and stood with ball-point poised. Sokolov said, 'It is the finding of this hearing that Victor Hopkins was shot by Merle Oates, a person known to this court to be of bad character and lengthy criminal background. It is the finding of this hearing that Merle Oates was shot by Petrus Berry, Retired Chief, Pinopolis, South Carolina PD, while in the act of illegally and without provocation discharging a firearm at the aforesaid Victor Hopkins and Mr. Hobart Lindsey.'

A cold wind swept along West 4th Street, bringing with it a horizontal spray of sleet particles.

'It is the ruling of this hearing,' Sokolov went on, 'that Chief Berry acted justifiably and correctly in discharging his firearm at the aforesaid Merle Oates. Have that typed up and ready for my signature asap, Officer. At Midtown North. Thank you.' She reached into her pocket, pulled out Berry's revolver, and handed it back to him. Berry checked it carefully, then slipped it into a concealed shoulder holster.

Sokolov said, 'Listen, fellas, it's colder than a eunuch's kiss out here. Let's head uptown. I'll get us a nice warm conference room and we can talk about this.'

She got them a ride in a cruiser. Officer Gulbenkian, of all the cops in the City of New York, drove them. When they got there they stripped off their outer clothing and settled down around a pot of coffee. Sokolov opened the conference by asking Petrus Berry for a suggestion. Lindsey felt miffed. It was his case.

' . . . this fellow Castellini,' Berry was saying.

'But we can't show any direct involvement,' Sokolov countered. 'Even if we take Bilbo Sax's word that Johnny Thieu Ng killed your brother and Frankie Fulton — which I doubt we could make stand up, even as a dying declaration — we know he was just an errand boy.'

'An errand boy with a gun,' Lindsey put in.

'Please,' Sokolov said witherngly, 'the chief and I are professionals. Okay?'

Lindsey frowned, then nodded.

'And we have Lindsey's statement that Victor Hopkins told him that Castellini runs mules to and from Europe to move art treasures.'

'How useful is that?' Berry asked. 'You don't even have Hopkins's dying declaration; you only have Lindsey's statement of what Hopkins told him. Not even good hearsay.' He patted Lindsey on the arm. 'Nothing personal. Just the way it works.'

Lindsey sighed. 'So you're saying we don't have anything we can use against Castellini?'

'That's exactly what I'm saying,' Sokolov said. 'Plus, Castellini nestles comfortably under the wing of Randolph Amoroso, our distinguished congressman from up in Dutchess County.'

Lindsey pushed his chair back angrily. 'You're telling me you're going to run around picking up corpses as long as they're just criminal scum? I guess it's okay that Millicent Martin is dead, because she was a mule for Castellini. Maybe. And what about Hopkins? And what about Cletus Berry? Is it okay they're dead because they were involved, somehow, with the little bad guys, but we don't dare touch the big bad guys?'

'Lindsey,' Sokolov said, 'I swear to you on my parents' graves that I will hang Alcide Castellini from Cleopatra's Needle in Central Park if I get the chance. But I'm not the X-Men, okay? You want a vigilante, I'm not it. I bent the rules like a pretzel tonight to keep Chief Berry out of trouble and let him keep his gun. I did it because he's one of the good guys. So I found a wormhole to scoot us both through.'

She was breathing hard, and there was color in her face that was not put there by the cold night air.

'But I tell you, and I want you to hear me: I cannot touch Alcide Castellini right now. If and when I can, I will. But right now, I cannot raise a finger against the man.'

18

Petrus Berry paced restlessly. Lindsey sprawled on a sofa. The third-floor living room of Zaffira Lazarini Fornari's flat overlooked a small garden in the rear of the brownstone. A set of French doors and a tiny balcony overhung the open area. A pair of trees stood in the garden; they had lost their leaves and stood stretching skeletal fingers into the night sky. Lower shrubs were coated with snow and the snow-covered ground reflected the moonlight, creating a spectral image.

An old-fashioned clock stood on the mantel; its filigreed hands showed three o'clock. Marcie Sokolov had sent them home from Midtown North in an unmarked car. 'I don't want to scare you guys — ' she started to explain.

Lindsey interrupted. 'What's to be scared of, just because that little creep Merle Oates tried to kill me?'

'I don't think he was trying to kill you,

Lindsey. You're just asking questions. But Victor Hopkins was giving you answers. That's what they didn't want.' She grinned. 'Of course, Merle wasn't trying *not* to kill you. As long as he got Hopkins, killing you would have been a little extra something for nothing. I'm glad that you're out of the Torrington Tower, and I'm double glad that you'll be bunking in with Chief Berry here. But just in case somebody's watching, I don't want to send you home in a cruiser. We'll send you fellas out through the garage in an unmarked car. Gulbenkian'll make sure there's no tail before he drops you off at your digs.'

Berry and Lindsey had agreed without discussion that neither of them was ready for sleep. Berry stood at the French doors, staring down into the white garden. From the sofa, Lindsey watched him. Each held a snifter of brandy. Zaffira Fornari had impeccable taste.

'I never thought I'd see my brother dead,' Berry said. 'I'm ten years older. Our parents are gone; I have nobody of my own. He should have buried me.' He shook his head sadly. 'It isn't fair and it isn't right.' He'd unstrapped his shoulder holster and laid it, the revolver in it still, on Zaffira's dining table.

Lindsey said, 'Petrus, I think Cletus's army service is the key to this whole thing. And that damn chariot keeps popping up in my mind.' He waved his hand vaguely, as if the chariot were floating through the air, or maybe flying over the snow-covered garden like Santa's sleigh. 'Didn't he ever tell you anything about Italy? About what he did there? Did he ever say anything that might have tied in with his death?' he asked. 'And all the others?'

Petrus shook his head. 'Ten years is a long time between children, Lindsey.' He frowned. 'I take it you think Alcide Castellini is behind the whole thing?'

'I do. And I think your brother's involvement started when he was in the army.'

Berry shrugged. He looked at Zaffira Fornari's antique clock. 'Quarter to five. Almost dawn. I'm going to hit the hay. I suggest you do the same. I'll set the

238

alarm. We'll get up and tackle this when our heads are clear.' He jerked a thumb toward a dark wood door. 'Linen closet.' He gestured again. 'Bathroom.'

'Got it,' Lindsey said.

'Eight o'clock okay?'

Lindsey blinked. 'Sure.'

'We'll consult the official family historian, Anna Maria. See what she has to say.' Berry disappeared into the bedroom and closed the door behind him.

★ ★ ★

When Lindsey and Berry arrived at the apartment, Zaffira Fornari took her sister out for a walk and a snack. International Surety's benefits package included a company-paid death benefit and a fat life insurance policy. The double-indemnity clause would apply, since Cletus Berry had been murdered. His family would not go hungry. Except for his presence.

'I wouldn't call myself a hacker.' Anna shook her head. She wore her hair in pigtails today, with bright red ribbons at the end of each. It was good to see her

239

out of black. She was amazingly bright, and this soon after her father's funeral, fairly cheerful. She didn't wear the mourning weeds that her mother and aunt did. Little Ezio sat on her lap, turning his head frequently to take in the conversation. 'But I can do a few tricks,' she added. 'You want to know about my father?' When she wasn't clattering away at the keyboard, she stroked the dog's shiny black-and-gold coat.

She had admitted them to her room and proudly showed off her up-to-date computer. 'I hacked into the Pentagon,' she admitted. 'That was so easy, it hardly even counts. They have all these software locks, but anybody who knows anything can open one in a minute.'

I ought to introduce her to Marty Saxon, Lindsey thought. *They're birds of a feather.*

'Do you want to see my dad's service record?'

'Very much so,' Lindsey said.

Anna looked at her uncle. Berry nodded silently. Anna said, 'All right, then. You'll have to give me a few minutes.'

Lindsey studied her room while she clattered away at the keyboard. She had posters on her walls and a row of Barbie dolls, one or two of them white, the rest dark brown. A long bookshelf ran from the closet door to the edge of her window. Half the shelf was filled with computer manuals. The rest of her collection seemed to be composed of history books and biographies of notables.

'Here it is,' Anna said. 'I have a copy on my hard drive, but I thought you'd rather see the actual Pentagon 201 file.'

'What's a 201 file?' Lindsey asked.

'Military personnel record,' Berry furnished.

They settled behind the girl. 'I can print this out if you want,' she said. 'I never did because I don't want to have any paper here that somebody could see and cop to what I'm doing.'

'Actually, a floppy would be good,' Lindsey said, 'and a hard copy, too. If you don't mind.'

'Sure.'

★　★　★

Cletus Berry had gone to the Infantry School at Fort Benning, Georgia, then to the Army Finance School in Indiana, and finally to the Army War College in Pennsylvania. That seemed odd for a warrant officer. Lindsey didn't know much military protocol, but he had the impression that a warrant officer was a pretty small character in the army's scheme of things. Why did Berry have these qualifications?

He'd been assigned to NATO headquarters in Brussels, then sent to Southern Command, assigned to Rome, with frequent visits to the NATO office at the Italian naval base at La Spezia.

Why did La Spezia ring a bell? Lindsey wracked his brain. Yes, La Spezia was the port where the *Fior di Rimini* had docked in 1940. The port where a cargo inventory had discovered the body of Massimo di Verolini in the crate that should have contained the missing Silver Chariot. And the port where the investigation was taken over by a fascist official swiftly dispatched from Rome — Salvatore Castellini.

There was something else peculiar about Cletus Berry's service record. His brother noticed it, and frowned. 'Look at that. Look at Cletus' discharge status.'

Lindsey complied. 'General discharge. What does that mean?'

'It means that Cletus was discharged from the army, um, how did they put it, it's been so long . . . under honorable conditions. But it's not an honorable discharge.'

'I don't understand that.'

'Well, an honorable discharge means you served your country and your enlistment had expired or your draft time was up or whatever. They give you a figurative gold watch and shake your hand and send you home.'

'And dishonorable?'

'Well, you punched out your CO or you stole a pistol from the armory and sold it off-post or — you see? You could be court martialed for what you did — they could send you to jail or impose some other penalty, and then when they were finished punishing you they'd hand you a *dis*honorable discharge. You couldn't get a decent job in those days with a DD. You didn't get any veteran's benefits. No GI Bill. No VA hospital. Nothing.'

'But look.' Lindsey pointed at the screen. 'He didn't get an honorable discharge *or* a dishonorable discharge. He got a *general* discharge. What does that mean?'

'What I told you. It means he was discharged under honorable conditions but he didn't get an honorable discharge. And it doesn't say why. Either somebody kept the reason out of his file or somebody cleaned it later on. Anna Maria — ' He put both his hands on the child's thin shoulders. ' — did you show your dad how to get into this file?'

'No. I was afraid I'd get in trouble, so I never told anybody I could do this.'

'Okay,' Berry said. 'He didn't do it himself. Either the reason was never there, or somebody else cleaned it out.'

A key grated in the front door lock and Ezio jumped off Anna's lap and ran from her room. His claws clattered on the hardwood floor as he sped to greet Ester and Zaffira.

Ester came into Anna's room and embraced her daughter. She gave her brother-in-law a chaste kiss, then shook Lindsey's hand. 'What are you learning?' Her voice was hoarse, her English almost unaccented.

'Mrs. Berry — ' Lindsey said.

'Ester.'

'Ester, we need to know more about what Cletus was doing in Italy. What he was doing in Rome.'

She shrugged angrily. 'He was an officer. He did as he was told. It was fifteen years ago. A lifetime ago. Look at me.' She held out her hands. 'I was a school girl. Ask Zaffira. She's older. She knows more. Ester Lazarini is dead. I am in the grave with my husband.'

Anna started crying. 'Mama, no.' She clutched her mother and buried her face in her chest.

'What was he doing in La Spezia?' Petrus Berry persisted.

'Out.' Ester Lazarini grasped her daughter with one hand and tore at her own hair with the other. 'Out!' she wailed. 'Out!'

19

'I blew it. I'm sorry,' Petrus Berry said. He and Lindsey walked westward on 73rd Street. A cold wind picked up and whipped their coats and stung their faces. 'Sometimes being a cop and being a human being don't jibe at all. How could I do that to those two girls?'

'It's done,' Lindsey said. 'Over. Give Ester a chance to calm down. We have to talk to Anna Maria again, and her cousin in Italy. What time is it over there? Halfway across the world, how do they talk to each other, Anna and Mosé?'

'I'll ask. I screwed it up and I'll fix it up.'

They crossed Fifth Avenue and turned downtown, skirting the low wall that set Central Park off from the broad sidewalk and the whole East Side.

'There's Anna's school,' Berry said. They'd reached 65th Street. The sun had finally burst through the grayness of the past days. The sky was a brilliant blue.

'It's too soon to get back to them,' Lindsey said. 'Let them mourn. We'll try later.'

They turned and walked across 58th Street. As they passed the Torrington Tower, Lindsey spotted Hassan Muhammad seated behind the guard desk. 'Petrus, just hold on a minute. I have a hunch.'

They entered the lobby. Hassan Muhammad looked at Lindsey, uncertain of who he was. Lindsey reminded him and Muhammad said, 'Yes, I have a letter for you.' He handed Lindsey a business-sized envelope. The International Surety crest was embossed above the return address, and in ball-point ink someone had added the initials MAZ. Morris A. Zissler.

Lindsey carefully slit the envelope. He scanned the contents, slipped the single sheet of paper back into the envelope, then tilted his head toward the lobby doors.

Once they were outside again, he headed toward the corner. Then he handed the letter to Berry. Without breaking stride, Berry read the note and handed it back to Lindsey. 'Who's Moe Zissler? And who's Cele Johnston? What's her point?'

'Zissler's a small-timer in International Surety. Cele Johnston runs an antique shop on 57th Street. She must have phoned Manhattan East because I gave her my card and it only has the Denver number on it. She must have called there and they told her I was in New York. So she looked — '

'Got it. This has something to do with the case, right?'

'Cele Johnston knows Alcide Castellini. The time I talked with her, she started to open up about Castellini. Then she changed her mind and practically threw me out of her office. Now she wants to talk to me again.'

'Right now? You think you ought to call ahead?'

'I don't think so. She got spooked the other time. Looks as if she keeps changing her mind. If she wanted to talk to me enough to phone International

Surety, I don't want to give her a chance to change her mind again.'

★　★　★

Cele Johnston gave Petrus Berry a suspicious up-and-down. Her eyes settled on the slight bulge under his left arm and she nodded, almost imperceptibly. Lindsey had introduced him by name, saying nothing about his relationship to the case. She offered Lindsey and Berry the use of a century-old coat rack and two cups of tea shimmering in translucent bone china. She said, 'You made the *Times*. Congratulations. Now all the best people will know about you.' She nodded toward Petrus Berry.

'I didn't see the paper today,' Lindsey said. 'Did you, Petrus?'

'Guess we're getting too wrapped up in our own doings.'

Cele slid open a drawer of her desk and laid a morning newspaper on the desk. It was already opened to a story about the slaying of Victor Hopkins and Merle Oates. Lindsey scanned the copy. It ran a

249

few paragraphs on an inside page. There was no photo. The story described the deaths of Oates and Hopkins, and went on to describe the unconventional hearing that exonerated Petrus Berry. How the *Times* reporter got that was a mystery all on its own. Maybe Amy Baines knew the answer. There was no mention of Hobart Lindsey, Cletus Berry or International Surety.

Cele leaned forward and raised her eyebrows. 'You're related to Cletus Berry, sir?' she said to Petrus.

'Brother.'

'Mr. Lindsey, I think you're out of your mind.' Cele snatched the newspaper from her desk and deposited it in a tooled leather waste basket. 'I think you should pack your bags and head back to Denver.' She shifted in her chair. 'Mr. Berry, my condolences on the death of your brother.'

He sat like a statue.

'Your being here complicates this. I'd expected Mr. Lindsey to come here alone.'

'Anything you have to tell me ... ' Lindsey said.

She steepled her fingers in front of her face. Finally she nodded. 'All right. Alcide Castellini wants to see you. Wants to see Hobart Lindsey. He didn't indicate any wish to see you, Mr. Berry. I don't think you would be welcome. I really don't.'

Lindsey said, 'When and where?'

Cele took a sheet of elegant notepaper in one hand and an equally elegant pen in the other and jotted a few lines. She folded the paper and laid it on the edge of the desk nearest herself. 'Mr. Castellini asks that you come alone. No companion. No weapon of any sort. No electronic devices of any sort. Do you understand what he's saying?'

'No wire.' Lindsey had never worn a wire. The only person he'd ever known who did was Celia Varela. She'd worn a wire in Berkeley and wound up with a different kind of wire around her neck, and her tongue purple and swollen and protruding from her mouth. 'Sounds like he's making himself safe from me. How safe am I from *him*?'

'Mr. Lindsey, if he wanted you dead you'd be dead right now.'

'Really.' Lindsey stirred his tea with a delicate silver spoon. 'What about last night?'

Berry interrupted, 'I'm not really happy, folks.' Lindsey could see that Petrus had his right hand inside his suit coat. 'I think maybe we should leave, Lindsey.'

'No.' Lindsey shook his head. 'Ms. Johnston is right. If Castellini wanted us dead, we'd be dead.' He turned toward her. 'But you haven't answered my question. What about last night?' He nodded toward the discarded copy of the *New York Times* with the Oates-Hopkins story in it.

Cele actually blushed. 'That was a mistake.'

What the hell *was* Cele Johnston? Lindsey wondered. At their first meeting she had seemed to despise Alcide Castellini, and also to fear him. She'd given Lindsey Castellini's telephone number — Lindsey had never used it — and hustled him out of her store, apparently in a state of near panic. Now she was acting as if she was Alcide Castellini's right-hand woman.

Lindsey reached toward the folded sheet of notepaper. Toward it, not for it. A subtle game of manipulation was taking place. If he reached for the note, he knew Cele had the choice of snatching it away from his outstretched fingers or of letting him take it. Instead, by holding his hand a few inches above her desktop, he was forcing her to place the notepaper in his hand.

She did, and shot him a coldly venomous look.

Lindsey wondered if he had needlessly made an enemy, and lost by winning.

★   ★   ★

They sat in a wooden booth over bowls of soup in a place on Broadway. Lindsey reached across the table and handed the sheet of notepaper to Petrus Berry. He watched Berry's eyes track as he read the brief lines.

Berry handed the note back to Lindsey. 'Very nice.'

'You noticed it, too.'

'No time. And no telephone number. Just an address.' Berry tore the corner off a hard roll and dropped it into his soup.

'Cele Johnston doesn't strike me as a careless woman,' Lindsey said. He slipped the note into his pocket organizer.

'Nor me,' Berry agreed.

'Then why would she write the note that way? Did she expect me to rush right over there? Do you know that address?'

'I'm a stranger here myself.'

'Last time I saw Cele Johnston, I was trying to track down Castellini. She gave me a card with his phone number on it. *A phone number.* I'd assume it was Castellini's, but maybe not.' He tucked into his own meal.

Berry asked, 'Did you call the number?'

Lindsey shook his head.

'Why not? If you're convinced that Castellini is at the center of this case . . . '

'I didn't know enough. I didn't want to go up against him until I was stronger. Until I was ready.'

'You're ready now?'

'I'm not sure. I've put together a lot of information.'

Berry signaled a waitress and ordered a cup of coffee. 'Lindsey, look here. We've got different methods. I'm a small-town cop. You're a big-time corporation man. I'm a pretty simple man, but I'll tell you I had a good record down in Pinopolis. And I guess you've got a record with International Surety. My brother never told me much about this SPUDS thing, but I know it's an elite outfit, and you would never make it into SPUDS if you didn't have plenty on the ball.'

Lindsey fidgeted.

'Or if you did,' Berry continued, 'and you didn't perform, you'd be out on your heinie in quick time. So I'm leveling with you.' His coffee had arrived and he added a drop of cream and stirred. 'Just what the hell do you have in mind? You don't intend to make a cold call on Castellini, do you?'

'I don't think so.'

'So you'll phone for an appointment, like a good little insurance man?'

Lindsey nodded.

'So let's plan this. You going in there alone?'

'Whatever.' Lindsey ate his soup.

'What are you going to say to the man? 'You killed my partner and I'm here to do something about it.' That it? He says, 'No, I didn't. Don't you read the newspapers? Johnny Thieu Ng killed your partner, and then the little freak-o checked out with a belt around his neck.' And you say, 'You killed Millie Martin.' And he says, 'Merle Oates did that, the little creep, and then he killed your pal Hopkins, and then your other pal Pete Berry killed Oates, and everything is nice and even-steven, case closed.' And he laughs you out of there.'

'What about the chariot? The mules? The Amoroso campaign?' The air in the restaurant was full of warm cooking odors. Suddenly Lindsey was sweating.

'What do you have, man?'

Lindsey's ears were ringing. 'What are you saying, Petrus? That Castellini is all right and that none of this is any of my business?'

'You might think about that.'

Lindsey took a generous sip of ice water. 'My company has fifty million bucks riding on this case.'

'Fifty *million*?'

Lindsey explained the Nyagic policy and Desmond Richelieu's calculation of the rebate International Surety stood to collect if IS could recover the chariot and return it to the Italian government.

'Oh, my, my.' Berry shook his head. 'So that's what it's all about. Damn, I should have known as much.'

'No, I wouldn't care if International Surety stood to make fifty cents instead of fifty million dollars. I'm in this for Cletus Berry. Period.'

There was a silence, filled with the clatter of silverware and dishes and the buzz of conversation all around them. Lindsey fumbled in his pants pocket, found a folded handkerchief, and mopped his forehead.

'Thank you,' Berry said softly. He picked up the check, reached for his wallet, and started toward the cashier.

'No need. This is on IS.'

They started down Broadway. Holiday shoppers were taking advantage of the clear day and the sidewalk was crowded.

A perfect setting for anonymous conversation.

'You don't think I should follow up with Castellini, then,' Lindsey said.

'I do. But I think you need more ammunition before you go face to face. And you need a plan, Lindsey. For heaven's sake, you need a plan. From everything I've heard and seen, Castellini is a chess player. He plans his game, he moves his pieces around, you see the pieces but you don't see him. He makes sacrifices. What do you think, Fulton, Ng, Sax, Merle Oates — they're all just pawns and he's lost them and so what? What does he care?'

They walked on.

Berry continued, 'Who are our pieces? We've lost Cletus. He was more than a pawn, Lindsey, he was a knight. We've lost Millie Martin and Victor Hopkins. Huh, and the poor fellow in the Torrington Tower, Bermudez.' He studied the sidewalk and kept moving ahead. 'And if your theory about Italy and the chariot is correct, I suppose even what's-his-name, Massimo — '

'Massimo di Verolini.'

' — right. Was the first piece to go. All the way back in 1940.'

'Okay. We're the good guys, Castellini's the bad guy, we've lost some pieces, he's lost some pieces. What now?'

'Now? Now I think we consider our options, Lindsey.' He nodded. They were in the West 40s, on a crowded corner. The light was against them and the cross-town street was packed solid with vehicles, mostly cabs, a few limos, and some daredevil messengers on bicycles.

'And there's one more thing we do,' Petrus said. 'We try to analyze our enemy's strengths and weaknesses and see if we can scope out *his* intentions. Question: What the hell is Castellini after?'

The lights changed and they maneuvered their way through a maze of halted vehicles.

'That's easy,' Lindsey furnished. 'He's after the chariot.'

'I think you're right.'

They reached the opposite curb, like explorers who had waded a stream and reached the farther shore undevoured by giant lizards and unpoisoned by aquatic vipers.

'And why is he after the chariot?'

'I don't know if he knows about the old Nyagic policy and the chances of getting that money back for International Surety.'

Berry frowned. 'You can be sure he knows about it. If he was working with Cletus, he knew about Cletus's place in the Torrington. If he's connected with our old Salvatore Castellini, which seems to be very likely, you can be damn sure he knows about the insurance policy. But he's not International Surety. How the hell could he profit from finding the chariot and turning it over to International Surety or to the Italian government? What's in it for him? Some dinky finder's fee? Hardly. And we know this man is no altruist. What the hell is in it for him?'

'Politics. Randolph Amoroso. The New Rome. And Benito Mussolini and *his* version of the New Rome. Salvatore Castellini. Alcide de Gasperi and Palmiro Togliatti.'

'You're losing me.'

'That's okay,' Lindsey said. His stride picked up. 'I don't know much about this stuff either, but I know somebody who does.' He dragged Berry along, cutting through the crowds.

'Who are you talking about?' Berry demanded.

'I'm talking about Mora Selvatica. Professor Blackberry!'

20

Anna Maria and Ezio were walking west on 73rd Street when Berry and Lindsey arrived, making their way from the IRT station at Lexington and 68th. Anna wore a knitted ski cap and a quilted jacket. Ezio Pinza wore a bright red dog-sweater.

'He's done everything,' Anna said. 'We were ready to go home anyway.' Her Uncle Petrus got a kiss. Lindsey got a handshake.

Lindsey said awkwardly, 'Anna Maria, I think we're making some progress on — '

'It's about your dad,' Petrus supplied.

Lindsey thanked him silently. 'You know the Silver Chariot you talked to Professor Van Huysen about, in your chat-group?'

'Yes.'

'Do you know how much that chariot is worth, Anna Maria? Do you know who would want it, and why?'

She shook her head. Her glossy black

hair poked out under the edges of her ski cap.

'What I was thinking,' Lindsey said, 'was, if we could get in touch with your cousin Mosé, maybe we could learn something more about the chariot.'

'It's just a history chat-group,' Anna said. She paused. If she didn't want to help, there was little Lindsey could do.

'Maybe *Dottore* Pacinelli would know,' she said.

Lindsey inhaled cold, clear air. They had reached Anna Maria's building. The dog seemed eager to get inside where it was warmer, and where he might have a doggy treat awaiting.

Lindsey thought he'd heard the name before but he couldn't put anything with it. 'Who is *Dottore* Pacinelli?'

'He's Mosé's teacher. He's his friend. He's a great scholar. He knows the whole history of the Jews in Italy, from ancient times to now.'

That was where Lindsey had heard the name before. Carlo Pacinelli, Ester Lazarini's childhood friend.

'Would Mosé ask *Il Dottore*?'

'Better.' Anna Maria managed a grin. 'What time is it, Mr. Lindsey?'

He told her.

'Mosé should be online in a little while. His parents are friends with *Dottore* Pacinelli. He visits them a lot. He might even be there now, or Mosé could telephone and he'll come over.'

★ ★ ★

She booted up and set up a chat with Mosé. *Il Dottore* was visiting Mosé's parents, Abramo and Sara. Mosé told Anna that they had shared their dinner.

Ester Berry and Zaffira Fornari had insisted that Anna Maria drink a cup of hot cocoa and put on warm socks and shoes before she did anything else. Ezio had devoured a charcoal bone and was curled up on Anna's bed with a bright yellow porcupine half his size.

Anna clattered away at the keyboard. Her message appeared in black letters on the monitor screen. Lindsey and Berry sat on kitchen chairs, one to either side. She hit *enter* and they waited for a response.

It came in seconds.

Dottore Pacinelli here. So sorry about your father. I write to your mother. Did she get my letter?

Anna told him she hadn't yet. But snail-mail, after all . . .

Si. posta di chiocciola. Please, tell to her my condoglianza.

Anna asked — Mosé? *Il Dottore?* — what they could tell her about the Silver Chariot. She explained that her Zio Pietro and her father's friend Signore Lindsey thought it held the key to the murder.

Una leggenda. Un mito. There was no such thing.

But there was. Lindsey was prepared to prompt the girl, but she needed no prompting. She wasn't just Anna Maria Berry. She was Mora Selvatica, or half of Mora Selvatica, and her cousin Mosé Lazarini was the other half, and they knew the history of the chariot as well as anyone, including William Van Huysen, Ph.D. But not — perhaps — as well as *Dottore* Carlo Pacinelli.

It took some coaxing. But eventually *Il*

Dottore gave a veiled history of the chariot, post-1940. All of this was speculative, of course. No one knew for certain. He could not swear, he would not publish his findings, his reputation as a scholar, his standing in the community . . .

It may have helped that Mosé Lazarini was his star pupil and was at his side at the keyboard. It may have helped that he was the onetime schoolmate and friend of Ester Lazarini. The embers of youthful loves glow stubbornly.

Some good fascist crewman aboard the *Fior di Rimini* had bashed in the skull of Massimo di Verolini not long after the ship had cleared the harbor at New York, those five decades before (*Dottore* Pacinelli said). Who had given him his orders? No one could even guess. What had become of him? No one knew. Long dead, probably, fighting the Allied invaders at Anzio in 1943, or fighting the Nazi occupation in 1944 when German armies rolled into Italy after the surrender, or fighting communist partisans in the streets of Rome or the countryside in

1945 when Italy lay in ruins and writhed, close to civil war.

And where was the chariot that should have been where instead was found the not-so-fresh remains of Massimo di Verolini? Somewhere on the ship. And when Salvatore Castellini, that good fascist functionary, hurried up to La Spezia from Rome and reported in horror that the sacred relic, the Silver Chariot, was nowhere to be found — what had really happened?

Chi conosceri? Lindsey could almost see the *Dottore*'s shrug. But he might guess. Yes, he might offer a conjecture.

Signore Castellini, he was a good fascist. Or maybe he was not such a good fascist. *Forse* — maybe — he had some ideals that were not the same as the party's ideals. *Forse* — maybe — he had some personal ambitions that were not the same as *Il Duce*'s ambitions.

It was not for sure, not *fidato*, but suppose Salvatore Castellini had been the employer of the crewman involved. Suppose his report to Rome had been false, a set-up. Suppose he had received the small crate containing the chariot, that had been intended to go in the large crate, and done — what? — with it?

If this story was true, this *nozzione*, this *teoria* . . . and if the chariot had survived the Allied bombings and the invasion from the south that followed, and the Nazi invasion from the north, and the turmoil and violence of the war . . . It was just *possibile* that it was still hidden away somewhere in Italy.

And, Lindsey thought, Alcide Castellini was looking for it.

And Cletus Berry, who had been in Italy as early as 1972 and as late as 1979; who had left the army under unspecified other-than-honorable conditions, and who later found the Nyagic file and got his brilliant daughter Anna Maria to unlock it for him . . .

Might very well have found the chariot.

Lindsey buried his face in his hands. Why would Alcide Castellini order Cletus Berry's murder?

Lindsey had thanked Mosé Lazarini and Carlo Pacinelli for their help. Before Anna logged off he also got their telephone numbers. Voice communication might be going the way of handwritten letters, and the day of keyboard-to-keyboard communication might be at hand, but Lindsey might want to talk with the Roman players in this game before everybody's vocal cords turned into vestigial organs. To Anna he said, 'Don't forget, International Surety will reimburse you for the online charges.'

Anna smiled wanly. 'Is that all? I think I want to play some games now.'

Lindsey rubbed his temples with his thumb and forefinger. 'One more thing, if you don't mind. You got your dad's 201 file. Could you get somebody else's 201 file?'

'Sure. What do you have for me to search on?'

'Will a name do?'

'It's something. But unless it's a really uncommon name, there are millions and millions of files there; a service number or a date of birth or anything else you could give me would be better.'

Lindsey pondered. 'Afraid I only have a name: Harry Scott.'

Anna groaned. So did Berry.

It took an hour, disposing of deceased Harry Scotts and Harry Scotts who were too old be to the right one. Then they found Harry Scott who had served from 1960 to 1980 and retired after 20 years of service. Spent his last three years on active duty at NATO Southern Command. Current address for pension checks, c/o International Surety, Rome, Italy.

Bingo!

'Can you go deeper into the files?' Lindsey asked.

'What do you want?'

He thought about that. He knew he was getting close to something vital. But it was likely to reflect badly on Cletus Berry. How much did he want to upset Berry's young daughter? He didn't want to inflict more pain on her than she had already suffered.

'Could you just pull up everything you can on Harry Scott and give it to me on a floppy? He works for the company, and I need to find out about his background.'

'*Schnecken*,' Anna said.

'What's that?'
'Piece of cake.'

★   ★   ★

Lindsey lay on Zaffira Fornari's living room couch, staring at the ceiling and trying to make sense of his investigations. Moonlight drifted through the French doors, providing cold illumination to the room. Zaffira's antique clock ticked softly, and if Lindsey listened carefully he thought he could hear Petrus Berry's occasional snore from the bedroom.

He'd booted up the floppy before he went to bed. Anna had got everything. Uncle Sam's secrets were a joke. And Harry Scott had a commendation in his file for snooping out a ring of American military personnel who'd been engaged in art racketeering in the late 1970s under the guise of NATO business. The commendation didn't mention any of their names, but the dates were right, the geography was right, the facts were right. Everything fit. Everything came together and made a picture of an accusatory finger that pointed straight at Cletus Berry. Sooner or later Lindsey was going to have to talk with Harry Scott, SPUDS Regional, Rome.

He looked at the antique clock on Zaffira Fornari's mantel. Then he did a quick computation, found the telephone, and put through a call to International Surety in Rome. The line clicked and hummed, and then he was speaking with a receptionist. Lindsey looked down into the motionless moonlit garden, imagining the receptionist looking out an office window in Rome at a busy, sunlit street.

He identified himself and asked to speak with Harry Scott, SPUDS. The receptionist must be a local hire; she spoke English flawlessly, but with an Italian overtone that was nothing short of charming. Mr. Scott was out of the office.

This was SPUDS business, most urgent.

Mr. Scott was on holiday, on vacation.

This couldn't wait. Where could Mr. Scott be reached?

Mr. Scott didn't leave any address or telephone number.

Lindsey pondered. Maybe Scott had a laptop and a modem. Maybe he'd check his email, even on vacation. Maybe — but he wasn't quite ready to give up with the receptionist. 'Do you know where he went on vacation? Did he ever go in past years and send a postcard to the gang at the office? Did he ever come back from vacation and show off his photos and his souvenirs?'

'No, he — oh, wait. I do remember. He sent a picture postcard from Pisa. The Leaning Tower of Pisa.'

'Good. That's good. He was staying in Pisa? Did he visit any other cities?'

'Sorry, I can't remember. I remember only Pisa, because he sent the postcard.'

After the call, Lindsey ransacked Zaffira Fornari's apartment until he found a world atlas. He found Pisa easily enough, and there was La Spezia, just a hop, skip and a jump away.

Got you, Harry Scott.

★   ★   ★

In the morning, Petrus Berry brewed coffee and scrambled eggs and toasted rye bread. A copy of the *New York Times* was spread on the kitchen table. Zaffira Fornari was a faithful subscriber. A photo on the front page showed a smiling, shiny-domed Randolph Amoroso and his wife emerging from Mass at a church in Little Italy. Amoroso was handing a miniature reproduction of the Silver Chariot to a priest while Mrs. Amoroso stood by, providing the standard politician's wife's adoring smile. The caption referred to Amoroso stumping Little Italy in search of support for his senatorial bid. Apparently he was getting plenty of it.

'You awake enough to make some decisions?' Berry asked.

Lindsey laid down the newspaper. 'This thing is starting to come together,' he said. 'Anna Maria's contacts in Italy — '

'I think so too.' Berry shoveled eggs onto two plates and set them on the table. 'Then you think the chariot is in Italy after all? It's been there since 1940?'

'And I think Cletus knew about it. I'm sorry, Petrus, I know you loved your brother — '

'Facts are facts.' Berry sat down opposite Lindsey and methodically loaded his fork. 'Keep on going.'

'Cletus got in some kind of trouble in Italy in 1979. We know that he made trips from Rome to La Spezia. We know he was studying Italian antiquities. That's how he first met Ester and Zaffira. And he kept running into them in museums and galleries.'

'Okay. I know that.' Berry drank his coffee.

'Here's what I think.' Lindsey bit his lip. 'I think he was mixed up with the trade in art and antiquities. There's still a whole catalog's worth of art that's been missing since the Second World War. What's in Germany, what's in Russia, what's in private collections, what was destroyed — we'll never know the whole story.

'I don't know if Cletus was mixed up with Castellini as long ago as 1979 or if they got together later. I don't know whether he knew about the Nyagic policy in '79 or if he just poked around the IS database after he got into SPUDS and stumbled across it by accident. More likely the latter. How would he know about Nyagic before he came to work for IS?

'Cletus knew where the chariot was, or at least he had a damn good idea. He was trying to sell it to Castellini. What could Castellini do with it? He could smuggle it into the US using his Omaha housewife dodge and sell it on the underground antiquities market. He could get a fortune for it. Or he could turn it over to Randolph Amoroso. That's what I think he was going to do.'

He paused. Berry looked up at him, coffee cup in hand. 'Why?'

'I think Amoroso wants to be more than a senator. He's got crazy ambitions. He wants to set up some kind of pseudo-fascist government. Rally all the old Nixon and Reagan types, the Gordon Liddys and the Ollie Norths, maybe tie in with some of those wild talk-radio characters. It sounds crazy; it's outside the bounds of American politics.'

Berry growled. 'You know what I think.'

'All right. But it could be a lot worse, Petrus, a whole lot worse.'

Berry glowered. 'Are you saying that Amoroso is the bad guy, or Castellini?'

'I think Amoroso wants to be an American *Il Duce*. Good God, he's even imitating Mussolini's style and his posturing. But I think Castellini sees Amoroso as a puppet. Castellini knows all about using fronts. Think of Omaha. Amoroso isn't a good guy, but he's a lightweight. Castellini is the danger. And Harry Scott — there's a wild card for you — Harry Scott is our man in Rome, and he's been snooping around La Spezia for years.'

'All right.' Berry heaved a sigh and pushed himself away from the table. 'You finished, Lindsey? I hate to waste food. Mama always told us it was a sin to waste food.'

Lindsey picked up his plate and finished his portion of scrambled eggs. 'I want to check in with Marcie Sokolov, but I don't think she's going to buy this. She's NYPD to the core; her feet are on the sidewalk. I don't think she'll buy my blue skies.'

'What then?'

'I'm going to bring my boss up to date. Cletus ever tell you about Desmond Richelieu?'

'J. Edgar Hoover, Junior?'

'That's him. But inside there's more to Richelieu than that. I want to go talk to Castellini. Depending on how that comes out, I may have to go to Italy.'

'You really think so?'

'You want to go along? I'd appreciate it, Petrus. Really.'

Berry shook his head. 'You know what, Hobart? You come on like Caspar Milquetoast, but inside that mild-mannered exterior lurks one crazy operator. Cletus told me how you hated to ever let go of a case, but he never told me that you could be one wacko individual.' He paused. 'And one dangerous man,' Berry concluded.

Lindsey said, 'I'll get SPUDS to start pulling wires. You have a passport? No? Neither do I. What do you bet that Desmond Richelieu can call some old buddies in Washington and have a pair of them in our hands tomorrow?'

'I don't bet.'

21

Petrus Berry didn't insist on taking two cabs, but he did insist on their paying off the cabbie and sending him on his way, a couple of blocks from their destination. Then they separated. Lindsey walked on to his destination. Berry refused to say where he was going or what he would be doing, but Lindsey suspected that he would be up to his old tricks again. Well, not so old, but still.

Lindsey had called the number Cele Johnston gave him at their first meeting. The voice that answered was neutral and so devoid of characteristics that Lindsey almost took it for a computer-generated signal. No gender, no age, no ethnicity, no emotion.

'A. P. C. Enterprises.'

That was what it said. The ball was in Lindsey's court. He asked for Alcide Castellini. The voice said that Mr. Castellini was regrettably unavailable, but if (he) (she) (it) could be of assistance, perhaps the caller would care to express his needs.

Lindsey stared at the telephone. He told the voice that Cele Johnston had given him an address and suggested that he visit Mr. Castellini, and he was calling to make an appointment.

The voice said, 'I see.' There was a lengthy pause. Then the voice said, 'If I may, please, ask your name, sir.'

Lindsey identified himself.

'Thank you. If you will hold for just a moment, sir. I do apologize for the inconvenience.'

Lindsey waited. At least there was no sappy music to tolerate.

'Mr. Castellini will see you at four this afternoon. Please observe the terms of visitation.'

And that was all. A soft click at the other end, and then silence. Lindsey knew enough not to phone again.

The day had been brilliant, and the city seemed more alive than it had at any time since Lindsey's arrival from Denver. The crowds were upbeat,

Christmas decorations were everywhere, and even the cab driver grunted a grudging thanks for his tip. He directed Lindsey to Gramercy Park in a strange language, but Lindsey found the house facing the charming little park, just off Irving Place. The cabbie had referred to it as 'Oiving's Place.' It was exactly four o'clock.

As Lindsey was about to press the doorbell, the door opened and Congressman Randolph Amoroso and his wife stepped out. Lindsey stared up at Amoroso. The congressman was struggling with his overcoat, trying to adjust a red-and-yellow plaid scarf. Lindsey took in Amoroso's trademark one-off clothing, his slightly-out-of-fashion suit, his shirt-collar just a trifle too long, his tie just the wrong shade and width.

Mrs. Amoroso smiled. She was not quite as far out of style, but her plain Republican cloth coat with its ratty fur collar could only offend a handful of anti-fur fanatics. Unless it was fake fur.

Before Lindsey could enter the house, the door swung shut. The Amorosos moved carefully down the short flight of stairs and away.

Lindsey pressed the doorbell. His pulse was racing and he could hear his own blood rushing and pounding in his ears. The house was surrounded by an iron fence, matching the fence that surrounded the park itself. The small lawn was covered with snow.

The door opened. A young woman in a severe outfit stood in the opening, looking businesslike and very much as if she was expecting something from Lindsey. Lindsey handed her a business card. Without a word she led him to a pair of tall, black-stained wooden doors fitted with gold appliances. The carpeting was richly patterned. The ceilings were tall and the architecture was ornate.

The doors closed behind Lindsey. Before him a middle-aged man sat at a desk. The room looked more like a gentleman's study than a business office, but the middle-aged man said, 'This is A. P. C. Enterprises. I am Mr. Campana. How may I serve you?'

Lindsey recognized the sterile voice. He

identified himself. 'I'm here to see Mr. Castellini.'

Campana nodded. 'You understand the terms. You have complied with them?'

'Yes.' Lindsey was astonished that Campana would take his word. That he had come alone was obvious — although he knew that Petrus Berry was somewhere nearby. But — no weapons? No wire? Maybe he'd passed through a detection device without knowing it. Or maybe Alcide Palmiro Castellini was simply above such things. You wouldn't shake hands with Alcide Palmiro Castellini wearing a buzzer ring, or hand him a drink in a dribble glass. Nobody needed to stop you. You just wouldn't do that.

Campana rose and led Lindsey to a second, grander pair of dark wooden doors. He knocked softly, waited, then opened the doors to let Lindsey through and departed, pulling the doors closed behind him.

This was a new realm. This was the headquarters of Alcide Palmiro Castellini.

Castellini himself stood beside an easy chair. He wore a dark-blue pinstripe suit that might have cost Lindsey a month's salary, a soft white shirt, and a solid maroon tie. His silvery hair had been razor-cut to perfection. He nodded formally.

Before Lindsey could say a word, Castellini motioned him to a chair similar to his own. A low table stood between them, and a third chair nearby. The walls were hung with paintings of the Italian Renaissance. Lindsey longed for a chance to study them. The little that he knew about art he had learned from his insurance work. He might not be able to identify the pieces, but he had seen a few authentic works of genius in his life, and he knew that such canvases glowed with a power as undeniable and as uneradicable as a radioactive isotope. Every canvas in this room glowed with that power.

'Would you like a drink, Mr. Lindsey? I would offer you a cigar, but my curator advises against smoke in this room. Or in the house, for that matter. It was designed by Stanford White. He himself lived here in Gramercy Park. A brilliant architect. Wild and self-indulgent. A sinner. Do you believe in sin, Mr. Lindsey? Hobart? May I call you Hobart? And you call me Alcide? Just not Al, please, I find that demeaning. If you'll grant me so much.'

Who was the chess-player, who the pawn?

Castellini eased himself into his chair and lifted a highball glass from the table. 'You are a remarkable man, Hobart. You astonish me.' He spoke English with that slight, cultured Italian that Lindsey was growing accustomed to. It was aristocratic, almost musical.

'No drink, no thank you,' Lindsey managed. He found himself fumbling for a prop. His laptop, his pocket organizer, his gold International Surety pencil. Determinedly, he folded his hands and placed them in his lap. Cele Johnston had been right. If Castellini wanted him dead he'd be dead by now. Consequently he need not worry about that. At least, that was what he told himself.

Castellini held a square, textured highball glass. The glass itself was clear. It contained ice cubes and a pale liquid. He lifted the glass and sipped, then placed it carefully on a coaster.

Lindsey looked around once more. The furnishings and art in the room were museum-grade, no question.

Castellini said, 'Congressman Amoroso was just here, Mr. Lindsey, with his lovely wife. You must have just missed them. What a pity.'

'I recognized him. We'd never met. Nor you and I. Mr. Castellini — '

'Alcide.'

'In honor of Signore de Gasperi?'

Castellini grinned widely. 'I didn't take you for so knowledgeable a man, but yes. And my middle name — Palmiro?'

'For Comrade Togliatti, I should think.'

'Bravo! The doing of my father. He followed Mussolini. Don't think ill of him, Hobart, for that. Most Italians followed Mussolini, at least at first. But once *Il Duce* was gone, well, who was going to win? The communists? The Christian Democrats? Who could tell? So my father named me for both, and whoever won, why, he was the namesake of Salvatore Castellini's son. What do you think of that, Hobart?'

'Opportunistic.'

Castellini grinned at that, showing beautiful teeth. 'I saw you at Cletus Berry's funeral, Hobart.'

'And I you.'

'*Sì, sicurati.* He was my friend. A fine fellow. We went back together many, many years. A tragedy. You're from his company; you've seen to his widow and his daughter? What a tragedy. I couldn't let them bury him without coming to show my respect. Very strange, a Jewish funeral — what do you make of that?'

'His wife is Jewish.'

'Ah, yes. I'm getting forgetful. There are so few Hebrews in Italy, one forgets. Perhaps Cletus took her faith. Did he ever speak to you of God, Hobart? Of religion? Only close friends discuss those things, don't you think?'

Lindsey blinked. This was getting out of control. He'd come to — why had he come here? He'd been pursuing Castellini so long, and now they were face to face. When Lindsey started the search he would have known what to say, but now everything had become so complicated, and Castellini was going on like an old buddy. Finally he asked, 'Did you kill him?'

Castellini looked distressed. Not angry, not surprised. It was as if a dear friend had accused you falsely of betrayal. You were saddened to think that someone of whom you thought so highly could think so ill of you.

'No.' He shook his head. 'No,' he repeated, 'Johnny Thieu Ng killed Cletus. Cletus and Frankie Fulton.'

'You paid him.' Castellini shrank as if Lindsey had reached toward him with a handful of some repellent substance, but Lindsey hadn't moved. 'What was your relationship with Millicent Martin?'

Castellini frowned in concentration, then brightened. 'Oh, you must mean Millicent Martinelli. What a calamity. Why do you ask about poor Millicent? What do you know about her?'

'I saw the newspaper photo of her with you and Fulton.'

'Ah, yes. I've learned to stay out of nightclubs.'

Lindsey was getting annoyed. He'd

come here ready to play chess, but the game seemed more like one of cat and mouse, and he did not enjoy playing the mouse. 'Was she your mule?'

'Who told you such a thing? She was — how to put this delicately? She was my protégé, yes?'

'You mean your mistress?'

'Protégé, mistress . . . there are other terms, euphemisms, some of them more polite than others. What do you prefer?'

'I didn't know her. I'm not involved.'

'Of course not. Then what does it matter? We traveled together. She was charming, vivacious. I am not as young as I used to be, Hobart. Her companionship was a joy. I didn't hide her. We appeared in public many times, many places, here and abroad.'

'Did you kill her, too?'

Castellini's face clouded. 'I'm starting to get annoyed, Hobart. Do you understand the seriousness of your charges? We're not talking about minor peculations. I could be very angry at what you're saying in private, and if you repeated these things in public you would be subject to a serious lawsuit.'

Lindsey clenched his fists.

'I will say one time and one time only,' Castellini continued. 'Your charges are absolutely absurd, and I will not waste more time on them. Now either drop your slanders or get out. I did not invite you here to be maligned. Do you understand me?'

Lindsey leaned forward. The situation was at once menacing and absurd. Here he sat in the lion's den. He'd called Castellini a murderer and Castellini seemed only mildly annoyed. If Castellini really was a killer, if he was directly or indirectly responsible for all the deaths that seemed to swirl around him, he would hardly hesitate to add one more.

The old Hobart Lindsey — the pre-Marvia Plum Lindsey — would never have dared act this way. He would have avoided Castellini, or tried to finesse him, or caved in and apologized. Instead he demanded, 'Why did you invite me here?'

Castellini relaxed. 'You've been looking for me.'

'Who told you that?' It had to be Cele

Johnston, Lindsey thought. Castellini had issued his invitation — or summons — through her.

Castellini said nothing.

'All right, Alcide.' He injected a microsecond of silence between the first syllable and the second, then instantly regretted it. It was a cheap shot. Castellini didn't notice. No, there was an extremely fine distinction to be made. He had not taken notice. 'I *have* been looking for you. Cletus Berry was my friend. I'm not satisfied with the police attitude. They're ready to write off his death as part of urban life. I want to nail the son of a bitch who killed my friend.'

'Mm, mm, mm.' Castellini drained the last of his highball. He rose and went to a small, inconspicuous bar. Over his shoulder he said, 'Hobart? Are you sure?'

Lindsey looked at his watch. What was the rule, never before six? 'All right.'

Castellini poured Lindsey a Scotch on the rocks, refreshed his own, and returned to his seat. 'Enough fencing. You may be trying to find Cletus Berry's killer. That's noble of you. You're also sniffing after

Caesar's Chariot. *Il Cocchio di Cesare*. So am I.' He paused and looked up at a fresco mounted on one wall of the room. Lindsey followed his gaze. By an odd happenstance, as little as Lindsey knew of Italian art, he recognized the fresco, a portrait of Angelo Ambrogini Poliziano, a fifteenth-century academic and writer, posing with Lorenzo de' Medici's son Piero. Why did Lindsey know the work? Oh, yes — there had been a flap in SPUDS when International Surety paid out the policy on the fresco, which had disappeared mysteriously and almost impossibly from the Sasseti Chapel in Florence.

Lindsey grinned behind his highball glass. He got control of himself and said, 'I don't have the chariot. I don't know where it is.'

'Cletus Berry did.'

'Then why did you kill him?'

Castellini glowered.

Lindsey rephrased his question. 'Why was Berry killed?'

'You aren't wearing a wire, Hobart. I'll tell you something you maybe shouldn't know. Certainly your friend Detective Sokolov doesn't know this and doesn't need to know it.'

Lindsey nodded. *I'm listening.*

'I worked with your friend Berry. I'm in the import business. I bring in goods from Europe, things of rarity and beauty, and sell them to those who will love and cherish them. I think of myself as one who facilitates the preservation of fragile treasures and their protection for the enlightenment of posterity.'

'Customs would have a different name for what you do.'

'Customs.' Castellini spat the word. '*Il Cocchio* has been missing since 1940. You know the story of *Il Cocchio*?'

'William Van Huysen told it to me.'

'Good. And you know about the World's Fair and the closing of the Italian Pavilion after the 1939 season.'

Before Lindsey could respond, Castellini stood up and moved toward the doorway. Lindsey thought he had heard a soft, almost inaudible chime, just before Castellini made his move. '*Scusi,* Hobart, a telephone call. Please indulge me.' He left the room.

Lindsey set his glass on a coaster. He rubbed his hand across his face. For the first time he became aware that the room was windowless. He was in Alcide Castellini's world, in a manifestation of Alcide Castellini's mind. There was neither day nor night here.

Castellini returned. 'Please, no more unpleasantness, Hobart. You deny knowledge of the whereabouts of *Il Cocchio*. Maybe you are telling the truth, maybe not. How much do you know about Nyagic?'

Lindsey could tell the truth, he could lie, he could say nothing. He told the truth.

Castellini nodded. 'You know more about Berry's work than anyone else. You understand his files. I think you can locate the chariot, even if you don't know now where it is. Find it. Give it to me. Not to your company. I will pay you — how much does your employer pay you in a year?'

Lindsey told him.

'At your present age, Hobart — you

know the actuarial tables — with promotions, with economic changes, your lifetime earnings — what do you think they would be?' Castellini named a figure.

Lindsey said that sounded about right.

'I will pay you ten times that amount. Cash, no taxes. I know how not to pay taxes.' He smiled. 'You resign from your job, you live out your life in the States or in Italy or in the country of your choice. You never lift a finger again unless you choose to.'

Lindsey picked up his Scotch and water, took a substantial drink, then lowered the glass. He stared at Alcide Castellini. The man did not look like Sydney Greenstreet, but he looked exactly like Sydney Greenstreet.

22

Credit Desmond Richelieu's old Washington connections for getting the passports as easily as phoning out for pizza, and Express Mail for delivering them faster than any pizza parlor chain that advertised on your local cable service. More astonishingly, credit Moe Zissler of Manhattan East for booking Lindsey and Petrus Berry on a quick flight to Rome. Lindsey had expected a struggle with Corporate Travel, having to use SPUDS clout to get what he wanted, and having to appeal at least to Richelieu himself and possibly higher in the corporate tower. He would have done so if he'd had to, to get Petrus Berry laid on as a short-term consultant at a dollar a day so he could fly with Lindsey on short notice and so International Surety would pick up the tab. But Moe Zissler, stolid and not very bright, had come through for good old International Surety.

Lindsey and Berry were seated side by side on an Alitalia 747. JFK was behind them, and it looked as if they might spend Christmas in Rome. Once the 747 left the ground, Berry managed to immerse himself in a paperback novel. Lindsey had no such power of inner tranquillity. Maybe he would gain that someday, but for him that day had not yet come. His mind kept circling around the case. He turned off the little light above his seat and closed his eyes. Faces floated into his consciousness as he tried to perceive connections and find meanings.

Cletus Berry, Millicent Martin, Johnny Thieu Ng, and Bilbo Sax. Cele Johnston, Victor Hopkins. Randolph Amoroso and his wife. Alcide Palmiro Castellini . . . and Harry Scott. The name without a face. Scott, who had served in NATO Southern Command with Cletus Berry. Scott, whose service record pointed straight to him as the whistle-blower who had ended Cletus Berry's army career.

But Scott was in Berry's electronic Rolodex. Had Berry never realized that

Scott was his own personal Judas? Had Scott maintained a bogus friendship with Berry all the years after betraying him to the army's criminal investigation division? And had Berry never seen through Scott?

Or had Berry realized at some point that Scott was his betrayer, and maintained the fiction of ignorance for purposes of his own? Were Scott's visits to La Spezia part of his quiet search for the Silver Chariot? And if they were, as seemed certain, was he acting on his own, or as Berry's stalking horse, or as Alcide Castellini's?

Lindsey had no idea they were going to be met at the airport. Rather than rent a car and attempt to drive on unfamiliar roads in a country where he didn't know the language, he planned to hire a car and an English-speaking driver. But there stood a middle-aged man dressed in houndstooth jacket and cloth cap, his leather-gloved hands holding a neatly lettered sign on a piece of corrugated cardboard: *International Surety — Mr. Lindsey, Mr. Berry*. Lindsey and Berry headed for the man.

The man greeted them with, '*Benvenuto a Italia, signores. Benvenuto a Fiumicino.*'

Lindsey stammered, '*No parlare italiano.*' He knew his grammar was terrible, but surely this fellow would get the idea.

The man threw his arms around Lindsey and Berry. 'Of course you don't speak Italian. Who could expect you to?' His English was perfect, American, with the flat twang of an Indiana farmer.

Lindsey said, 'Who are you?'

A bellow of laughter. 'Why, I'm Harry Scott. Got back into town last night. Found a stack of message slips on my desk this morning. *Call Hobart Lindsey. Call Hobart Lindsey, SPUDS.* Whatever Ducky Richelieu wants, Ducky Richelieu gets. *Call Hobart Lindsey, SPUDS, urgent!* Oh, so I tried SPUDS in Denver and tracked you to Manhattan East and spoke with a fellow named Zipper — '

'Zissler?'

'That's the name, Moe Zissler. He said you were already on a jet headed for Leonardo. Fumiano, the natives call it hereabouts. So I thought I'd just truck on down to the airport and pick you fellows up. Say, you don't look as jet-lagged as I thought you might. Feeling all right? Hungry? Thirsty? Need a hotel? Got a reservation? Harry Scott at your service.'

Lindsey said, 'Zissler made reservations for us. We're at the — ' He fumbled for his pocket organizer. ' — the Hotel Villa del Parco.'

'I know it well. Via Nomentana, lovely old place. Nineteenth-century. Tiny establishment, couple of dozen rooms, *tres intime*, gorgeous furnishings. You'll have a great time. How long you in town for? Zissler didn't know. Or he wouldn't tell me, anyway. He's cagey, that one.' He gave a hearty laugh. 'Listen, there's no need to stand here in this drafty terminal. It is December, you know.'

Scott drove a tan Alfa-Romeo. Lindsey found himself sinking into the soft upholstery. The roadway leading from the airport to the city was broad and smoothly paved, packed with shiny new cars intent on reaching their destinations at top speed and at any cost.

Before they had reached the car,

300

Lindsey and Berry had introduced themselves a little more formally to Scott. 'You related to — ?' Scott asked Petrus Berry.

'My brother.'

'Shame. Tragedy. Tragedy and a crime. I learned about it over KlameNet/Plus. Must really have shaken SPUDS and pierced Ducky Richelieu to the quick. He's a tough cookie, but he cares for his boys and girls. Uh, men and women.'

A white Volvo limousine, windows tinted opaque, whizzed past them so fast that its slipstream shook the Alfa.

'Skillful driver,' Harry Scott commented. 'Can't say I admire his attitude, but I can't fault his skill.' He shifted subjects without missing a beat. 'What are you fellows doing in Rome? I know you're SPUDS, Lindsey, but what about you, Berry? You part of the team now?'

'Temporarily.'

'Well, welcome, even if it is temporary.'

They entered the city as dusk was falling. Southern Europe was enduring a severe winter, and snow banks lined the streets of Rome. The city was decorated for Christmas just as New York was. Under other circumstances, Lindsey would have loved to play tourist. If Marvia Plum and young Jamie Wilkerson were with him, it would have been the best Christmas of his life.

They weren't, and it wasn't.

Scott switched on the Alfa's headlights. 'We're almost there, fellows. Say, I'll check you in, and then I'd love to stay but I'm afraid I have an appointment. The wife, you know — mustn't keep her waiting first night back in town. But if you fellows need a recommendation for where to get some tolerable eats, maybe I can help out. Unless you're too jet-lagged for a meal?'

'I'll sleep later,' Petrus Berry said. 'I'm too keyed up to think of turning in yet.'

Lindsey had no quarrel with that. Instead, he asked Scott how he had come to welcome them by speaking Italian.

'Married *una bella signorina*. Luckiest day of my life. I came to Italy a confirmed bachelor, a friend at the office introduced me to Giulia Pazzi, and I knew it was all up. Married her first chance I got.'

'So you learned Italian from your wife?'

'My darling *moglie, sì. Italiano*, even English. You know, I'm a farm boy. Little town in Indiana, you never heard of it.'

Bingo!

'Pazzi's are an old Italian family. Educated. Giulia learned her English at Cambridge, I'll have you know. Think I've picked up some of her mannerisms. Don't know what they'll make of me if I ever get back to Connersville. But I know what they'll make of Giulia — what a knockout, that's all they'll have to say about my darling bride.'

Scott pulled the Alfa to the curb in front of the Villa del Parco. The hotel lived up to his description. Lindsey and Berry shared a room overlooking the via Nomentana. Full night had fallen by the time they unpacked their bags, and by that time Harry Scott had piled back into his Alfa and headed home to his beloved *moglie*.

Lindsey looked up a couple of telephone numbers in his pocket organizer. He studied the Italian telephone. It wasn't too different from the American variety. He crossed his fingers and punched in a number.

'Pronto?'

Lindsey introduced himself, praying that there wouldn't be too much of a language problem. 'Is Signore Lazarini there? Signore Abramo Lazarini? This is Hobart Lindsey, of International Surety.'

'Si, yes, I am Lazarini.'

Lindsey told Lazarini that he was in Rome with Petrus Berry, the brother of Cletus Berry.

'I know, I know.' Lazarini had a heavy accent but Lindsey could understand him well enough. 'I know all about Cletus. You Americans, the crime in your country, so terrible. I try to get my sisters to come back to *Italia*, bring the little Anna Maria, but they won't come. Now maybe they come.'

Lindsey tried to explain their mission in Italy.

'I know everything. Mosé learns everything from his cousin. The *ragazzi*, the children, they know everything these days. What time, oh, you come here. Did you eat? No? Come, Lindsey and Petrus Berry.'

Lindsey jotted down the address. He asked if it was anywhere near the home of Carlo Pacinelli.

'Pacinelli? *Il Professore?* He is the neighbor. You want to speak with *Il professore?* I invite him too. You come ahead. Come now.'

Lindsey set down the telephone and grinned at Berry. 'Talk about hospitality.' He described his conversation with Abramo Lazarini.

'I got most of that,' Berry replied, 'from your half. I think there's more to it than just hospitality. Something that the *signore* maybe didn't want to talk about on the telephone.'

★   ★   ★

The concierge got them a taxi and the driver recognized the address that Lindsey gave him. He had some English. It seemed that everybody in Italy did. 'Via del Portico d'Ottavia, *si*, you go to ghetto *ebrei*. You try the *Carciofi alla Giudia*. Most best food in *Italia*.'

How this driver avoided one accident

after another was a mystery, but he delivered them to their destination without a scratch. The Via del Portico d'Ottavia took a dogleg toward the Lungotevere de Cenci and the Tiber. The taxi dropped them at the house of the Lazarinis. It looked as if the family had indeed lived there for generations.

Lindsey and Berry had discussed their agenda for the evening. In part the visit would be social, a sort of reverse condolence call in which Berry and the Lazarinis would discuss the tragic death of his brother, their brother-in-law. But Berry suspected there was more to the matter. The Lazarinis' son and his friend *Il Professore* would play a role. Berry suspected that they could contribute something to their quest for the Silver Chariot.

Lindsey considered that. 'What about Carlo Pacinelli?'

'What did Lazarini say about him?'

'He said, ah, 'Pacinelli is the neighbor. I invite him too'.'

'Just like that, eh? Not Lazarini's idea at all, was it? What do you bet, if you hadn't asked about him, *Il Professore* would have dropped in while we're visiting to return a borrowed frying pan, or something equally innocent?'

Once a cop . . .

Abramo Lazarini welcomed Lindsey and Berry at the door of their home. There was something about the man's eyes, something about the cheekbones, that Lindsey had seen in the faces of Ester and Zaffira — and Anna Maria. Lazarini ushered them into the living room. The furnishings were comfortable but they looked like something out of the 1920s: plush sofa and overstuffed chairs; a Persian carpet on the floor; a few framed prints on the walls; a lovingly polished menorah on one table, surrounded by family portraits.

Here Lindsey and Berry met the Roman branch of the Lazarini family. And *Il Professore* Carlo Pacinelli. Pacinelli was just a pleasant, slightly stuffy academic approaching middle age. A bachelor, presumably, visiting the home of a star pupil, meeting some foreign visitors, and getting a free meal out of it in the bargain.

Abramo Lazarini wore a black suit, a frayed white shirt, and a gray tie. In the light of the room, despite the difference in age, the family resemblance was even more striking. Sara Lazarini was more generously proportioned than her husband, and obviously younger. Her thick, dark hair was graying. She wore a black dress with white trim, a small gold Star of David on a fine chain, and a floral-printed apron. As a girl she might have been voluptuous; in early middle age she looked comfortable with herself and her world.

Recorded classical music provided a background for conversation. There was no sign of Mosé Lazarini.

Sara Lazarini retreated to her kitchen, nodding in time to the music. Her husband looked from Lindsey to Berry and said, 'You must see Rome. Everything is here. The museums, the statues, the paintings. I have traveled. Never to America, but to *Francia*, to *Grecia*, to *Spagna*. You must see the *Europa*. But the most beautiful is the *Italia*.'

Berry said, 'I've been to Okinawa.'

Lazarini raised his hands. '*Scusi?*'

'Never mind. I'm sure it doesn't compare.'

Lindsey said, 'I'd love to visit Italy again to see the treasures. But Mr. Berry and I are not here for pleasure. Not this time.'

Lazarini nodded solemnly. '*Sì*, I understand. So, you tell me why you come to *Italia.*'

Berry flashed a look at Lindsey, then said, 'We think someone killed my brother because he knew where Caesar's Chariot is. Lindsey has been investigating the case since the day they found Cletus's body. I'm working with him.'

Abramo nodded, then said something to Carlo Pacinelli in rapid Italian. While he spoke, Sara returned. Cooking odors swept from the kitchen along with her.

Abramo served wine. '*Bi'teh, Sara, inglese, inglese,*' he said. '*Bene, gueleebt, bene.* For dinner, you wait and see.'

Pacinelli nodded to Abramo, answered him briefly and as rapidly as he has spoken, then said, 'You know who killed your brother, Signore Berry? Some

American gangster, American mafioso?'

'Lindsey knows more about that than I do.'

Lindsey said, 'Do you know of a man called Alcide Palmiro Castellini? Born in Italy, now living in America.'

Both Lazarinis looked blank, but Pacinelli raised his hands in a gesture of surprise. He wore a gray tweed jacket, a white shirt, and a maroon knit tie.

'Wait, I will fetch young Mosé, please. He knows everything I know. We are scholars together.' Pacinelli disappeared down a narrow corridor.

A boy appeared in the doorway followed by Carlo Pacinelli. They advanced into the room. Sara wrapped her arms around the boy. '*Dammi un'abbraccio, miene liebling.*'

The boy looked at Lindsey and at Berry, then walked up to Berry and shook his hand. 'I am Mosé Lazarini. You must be the uncle of my cousin, sir.'

Lindsey heard an odd sound as Berry released the boy's hand and crushed him in a bear-hug. Tears were rolling down Berry's face. No one spoke. When Berry released the boy he said, 'I'm sorry.' He pulled a handkerchief from his pocket and wiped his face. Then he gave a little shudder and said, 'I'm okay now.' Still there was an embarrassed silence.

Mosé Lazarini stepped up to Lindsey and shook his hand. The boy did resemble his cousin Anna Maria. His short hair was black and wavy. His skin was a Mediterranean olive, darker than Lindsey's but lighter than Anna Maria's.

'How do you do, sir,' Mosé said. 'You must be Signore Lindsey. I've heard about you from my cousin.'

Lindsey nodded. 'I know Anna Maria. You must be the other half of Professor Selvatica.' Lindsey saw that Berry had recovered from his momentary breakdown and was directing his attention to the conversation.

Mosé laughed. 'Yes, sir. Professor Blackberry at your service.'

Sara Lazarini informed the room that their meal was ready. They went to the table. Meatloaf with hard-boiled egg, beets and noodles. It was delicious.

Carlo Pacinelli finally got his chance to

respond to Lindsey's question about Alcide Castellini. He did so by prompting his prize pupil, Mosé. 'You know of the Castellinis, *il padre ed anche il figlio*. You speak, Mosé.'

The boy wiped his mouth with a napkin. This was his chance to show off his learning in the presence of his family and his *professore*. He cleared his throat. '*Professore* Pacinelli and I, we study this. We have gone to La Spezia.'

Everybody was going to La Spezia. First the old fascist Salvatore Castellini. Then, Lindsey guessed, Cletus Berry. Harry Scott, and now Professor Pacinelli and his pupil Mosé Lazarini. 'It's still a port, then?'

'Very important. Venizia, Genova, Napoli, our famous ports. But La Spezia is very important, yes.'

'And were you able to trace the Silver Chariot? Can you connect it to Salvatore Castellini and Alcide Castellini?'

'*Si*,' Mosé said proudly.

'*Si*,' Carlo Pacinelli echoed his pupil. '*Certamente*.'

And Abramo and Sara Lazarini, in

unison: '*Gue'vis.*'

Lindsey and Berry exchanged a look. There was no way the child could have learned this much on his own, but he was a bright student and his *professore* prompted him, calling him back from false trails and filling in omitted details. It was soon clear to Lindsey that Professor Blackberry was more than the figment of Anna Maria Berry and Mosé Lazarini. Carlo Pacinelli, perhaps without knowing it, provided the biggest part of Blackberry's data bank. *Il Dottore* Mora Selvatica spoke with the words of two bright children, but with the thoughts and knowledge of a middle-aged scholar.

As young Mosé spoke, prompted by questions from both Lindsey and Berry and with his answers amplified by *Il Professore* Pacinelli, Lindsey jotted notes in his ragged pocket organizer. 'Italy has an ugly past,' Mosé asserted.

His father frowned but the boy continued.

'My people, we *Ebrai*, we Jews — we are part of Italy forever.'

He was echoing words that Lindsey

had heard in the 73rd Street apartment from Ester Lazarini. Lindsey tried to imagine being part of anything forever.

'We give Italy our love, and what does Italy give us?'

Later, Lindsey would amplify his notes into a report to Desmond Richelieu. But now he sat spellbound by the child's story.

23

Benito Mussolini had the support of the majority of the Italian people (Lindsey paraphrased the boy in his long memorandum to Desmond Richelieu), at least in his early years in power. That included Italian Jewry. Mussolini was no racist, certainly no anti-Semite. Italy had been in a state of political confusion and economic turmoil in the years following the First World War, and *Il Duce* was seen as a unifying leader who would bring discipline and order to the nation.

In power for a full decade before Adolf Hitler became chancellor of the Weimar Republic, Mussolini considered Hitler a petty upstart. The first time Hitler tried to grab Austria, Mussolini massed Italian troops and threatened war, and Hitler backed down. *Il Duce* was a hero to the British and French then. But the balance of power shifted. Hitler grew stronger. He and Mussolini became de facto allies in their support of Francisco Franco's falangists in the Spanish Civil War, and once their alliance was formalized, Mussolini began to toe Hitler's racial line.

The first modern racial laws were not proclaimed in Italy until 1938, and even then they were never as severe as those in Germany. Jews were precluded from entering certain professions, for example, but even then exceptions were made for decorated soldiers of past wars and for other distinguished individuals.

As the situation worsened and the Second World War progressed, Italian racial laws grew more stringent. There were concentration camps; but even these, as severe as they were, came nowhere near the horrors of the Nazi death camps. It was only with the fall of the Mussolini government, the surrender to the western Allies, and the invasion of Italy by German armies that wholesale arrests and deportation of Jews to the extermination camps began. There were attempts by some Italians to protect their Jewish brethren. Other Italians sold Jews to the Germans like so many cattle.

Flash back to 1937. Salvatore Castellini, early supporter of Mussolini and later Fascist Party hack, marries his childhood sweetheart. Blonde, blue-eyed, delicate-featured, she looks neither Italian nor Jewish. Even her name, Anna Schoenberg, sounds more German than either Jewish or Italian. But in fact Anna is a Jew; she is a distant cousin of the composer Arnold Schoenberg.

A year later, Mussolini announces the first of his anti-Semitic laws. Salvatore Castellini begins to worry. He is no beast; he is a sincere fascist. He believes in discipline, unity, nationalism. But part of that unity and nationalism is based on the conviction that all loyal Italians are potentially good citizens of the state. Now Jews are proclaimed aliens in their own land. *La Signora Castellini* is in danger. So is her entire family, and, by association, so is Salvatore Castellini. Italian Jews — and non-Jews who cast their lot with them — had better prepare for hard times.

Castellini finds himself assigned to the security apparatus of the Fascist Party and State. He becomes a member of OVRA — the *Operazione di Vigilanza per la Repressione dell' Antifascismo* — and two years later his opportunity arrives. World War II has broken out. The Italian Pavilion at the World's Fair in New York has been closed. The artifacts and treasures on display are returning to Italy aboard the *Fior di Rimini*, and when word reaches Rome of suspicious doings aboard the freighter, OVRA springs into action.

Salvatore Castellini uses all of his considerable cunning to get the assignment for himself; and when the disappearance of the *Cocchio* and the presence of the body of Massimo di Verolini are discovered, Castellini is the investigating official. The small crate containing the *Cocchio di Cesare* is smuggled off the *Fior di Rimini* by the one man positioned to commit the crime . . . the official sent by Rome to prevent the commission of the crime . . . Salvatore Castellini.

Or was it? The death of di Verolini, the disappearance of the chariot, and OVRA investigation under the care of Salvatore

Castellini — these are all verifiable occurrences. These were duly recorded at the time, and the records survive. But did Castellini actually take the *Cocchio*? This is not verifiable, only inferential. But the pieces all fit together, and the evidence all points to Salvatore Castellini.

Lindsey finds himself thinking of Dorothy Yamura's memorable dictum about coincidences. If not a proven fact, then as a likely hypothesis, Salvatore Castellini had possession of that toy in the early days of 1940. But he was unlikely to lug it around with him; the chariot would be far too dangerous. He would have had to put it somewhere or send it somewhere, deposit it somewhere. Where does the fascist Castellini, the husband of Anna Schoenberg, this man torn between two loyalties . . . Where does Salvatore Castellini deposit the chariot?

In the hands of the Jewish anti-fascist underground in La Spezia. For as Mussolini had turned increasingly against the Jews of Italy, the Jews of Italy had turned increasingly against Mussolini;

and the underground, itself a bizarre alliance of Jews, liberals, and Communists, is strong and well-organized.

Italy is already involved in the war, and things at first go swimmingly. But as the tide of battle slowly turns, the chariot is moved from hiding place to hiding place. For a time it remains in La Spezia. The principle of the Purloined Letter applies. Then it is transported to Bologna, where it comes to rest in a storage room in the City Hall. When bombs fall, it is moved, this time to Ravenna, where it is actually loaded onto a ship, the *Giovanni Acuto*, bound for Trieste, just across the Adriatic Sea. But the ship never leaves port. A stray artillery shell fired by a German garrison strikes the *Giovanni Acuto*, and only the quick action of an anonymous crewman prevents the *Cocchio* from disappearing into the murky harbor-bed.

The chariot makes its way as far south as Pescara, then across the width of Italy to Rome, where it falls into the hands of a group of Jewish anti-fascists, who hide it in — of all places — a catacomb beneath the sub-basement of the Great Temple — the splendid, extravagant synagogue that even the Nazis were too awed to destroy.

The Italian fascists, for all their ambivalence, never executed a full-scale pogrom against Italy's Jews. But once the Nazis took over, the full ferocity of a dying beast was unleashed. In Rome alone, more than 2,000 Jews were rounded up and shipped to concentration camps. Two thousand, out of a tiny population. Not all of them died in the camps. Records show that as many as fifteen individuals survived the camps and returned to Rome.

The insurance claim against New York Amalgamated Guarantee had been filed in timely fashion, as early as 1940, while Italy and the United States were still at peace, but it became obvious that it would not be paid while the nations were at war.

By the time the war ended, Italy was in ruins and in chaos. As for the chariot . . . no one knows where it is. No one knows whether it even exists any longer.

Lindsey and Berry had been on the edge of their chairs, resisting the urge to interrupt. At length Lindsey yielded. 'Pardon me, Mosé, but for a boy of ten, how do you know so much about these events, going back fifty or sixty years?'

'I have studied, sir.' The boy seemed sure of himself. '*Il Professore* and I, we study, we research. There are records. And there are stories. I swear you, sir, I tell you truth.'

Lindsey nodded and settled back in an ordinary wooden chair that might have hosted a Jewish owner in the 1930s, an Italian fascist by 1942, a Nazi trooper in '43, a Communist partisan in '44, a GI in '45, and its Jewish owner again by 1946.

As a matter of fact (Mosé resumed his narrative and, later, Lindsey his paraphrasing), the chariot was fifty feet beneath the Grand Temple, still in its packing crate.

Lindsey had his doubts. Through decades of clandestine searches, if the records existed and the chariot was indeed where Mosé claimed, would it not have been recovered long since? Still . . .

And what of Salvatore Castellini and his wife, Anna Schoenberg? In the chaos of war and the internal strife that wracked Italy even before Mussolini's downfall, Castellini had risen to the rank of major in OVRA, and had been able to offer protection to his wife by passing her off as a German Catholic.

In 1945, with the struggle between communist and anti-communist forces beginning in Italy, Castellini offers his services to the American military. He knows the secrets of OVRA; he knows where the bodies are buried — he is a valuable man. The army refers him to G2, military intelligence, which refers him to the Office of Strategic Services.

Under the protection first of the Americans, then of the Italian Christian Democrats of Alcide de Gasperi, Salvatore and Anna live comfortably in a fashionable apartment on the Via del Carrozze. Castellini's background — shadowy at best — should not bode well for him, but the Cold War is getting under way and both the Western and Eastern camps are known to hold their noses and put former Axis intelligence officers to use in their own burgeoning clandestine services.

In 1947 Anna gives birth to a son. Because Italy's political future is still in doubt, the proud parents name their baby after the leaders of the nation's two great political factions. Little Alcide Palmiro Castellini grows up in the gray world of dubious undertakings, ambiguous characters and black-bag operations. By the time he is 25 years old he has become friends with an American warrant officer named Cletus Berry and Berry's boss, a lieutenant colonel named Harry Scott.

Castellini has a reputation in the Italian shadow world. He has inherited his father's penchant for unsavory doings and dangerous associates, and his mother's unquestioned brilliance and artistic tastes. He is a man with no friends. He is also a man with few enemies, for those who interfere with his work are seldom seen for very long.

The Americans Cletus Berry and

Harry Scott work with Castellini the younger in an illicit exporting business. When some army investigators start sniffing around the operation, Scott sacrifices Berry to save his own hindquarters.

The result: Berry winds up with a general discharge from the army. As far as I can tell (Lindsey interjected in his memorandum) Cletus never did find out who blew the whistle on him. And Berry winds up working for SPUDS. Harry Scott wins himself a commendation for betraying his partner and takes early retirement from the army. Alcide Castellini becomes an American citizen and buys a magnificent Stanford White townhouse in Gramercy Park. All three partners continue working together — until Cletus Berry is shot dead in an alley in Hell's Kitchen.

And where is the *Cocchio di Argento*?

★　★　★

Carlo Pacinelli looked at Lindsey and Berry. They were seated facing each other at the dinner table. The meal had long since ended. Strong coffee had been drunk and lemon babka honey schnecken consumed. The music had ceased to play, and the only sounds other than conversation were those of traffic in the Via del Portico d'Ottavia, and the occasional bark of a dog.

Where was the Silver Chariot?

'No one knows,' Pacinelli said.

Lindsey pointed out, 'Mosé said the chariot was beneath the Grand Temple.'

Pacinelli smiled. 'Perhaps. A legend. A myth. The Golden Fleece of Perseus, the Holy Grail, the *Cocchio di Argento*.'

'Then how do you know so much about it? The whole story . . . ' Lindsey didn't know whether to be amazed at this windfall of information or furious that so much was known and nothing done about it.

Pacinelli said, 'I have devoted my life to this research. My people — my nation — are guilty of terrible crimes. Too much we hide them and pretend evil things never happened. But I want to know everything. I want to expose everything.

Only when everything is displayed in bright sunlight can Italy's conscience be clear.'

Lindsey saw that Pacinelli was gripping the edge of the table. His fingers were as white as the cloth from the pressure he placed on them. 'That still doesn't answer my question,' Lindsey persisted.

'In the files of the Jewish community of Rome. In the records of the Grand Temple. The rabbis, the congregation, they let me in. They call me their *giusto pagano*. They are very kind to me, very helpful. When I was a student they gave me a job. I was the beadle, the *shabbas goy*. I would perform the little tasks that a Hebrew could not on the Sabbath.' He grinned as if recalling a pleasant memory.

'And in the archives of the Memorial to the Jewish Martyrs. I searched there too. They have records. And in the Ministry of Justice, where the OVRA files have gone. They were not so pleased in the Ministry, when they learned what I wanted. There was still pressure, you know, from the Americans. But now the Americans are not so much afraid of communists, so they do not press the Ministry; and I have my degrees, my esteemed academic rank. *Dottore. Professore.* They think I am not interested in politics or in crime, just in history. So they let me search for facts.'

This was exactly the kind of information that Lindsey needed in order to make sense of this case. But Pacinelli was so glib, so forthcoming, so genial. How had this information found its way into those archives? Lindsey asked, and Pacinelli's forehead darkened.

'Anna Schoenberg wrote her memoirs and donated them to the Memorial,' Pacinelli said. 'In all the documents, she never refers to the chariot by name. She refers to it only by its crate number on the *Fior di Rimini* bill of lading, from 1940. It is only crate number 18 in all the documents. Only crate number 18.'

'Her husband kept her safe all through the war?' Lindsey asked.

'No.'

'She was finally caught by the Nazis, then?'

'Yes. She was sent to Dachau. She was one of the thousands rounded up and transported; one of the handful who returned.' He pressed his forehead against the upraised palms of his hands. 'When she came back, Salvatore Castellini welcomed her. They lived together. They had a son. All the while she was working with the archivists, documenting the horrors of the war.'

Lindsey asked, 'How did the Nazis capture her? You said she was married to a Gentile; she was passing as a German Catholic.'

'Yes.' Pacinelli paused. 'The story. The Germans were suspicious. Salvatore Castellini, OVRA Major Castellini, was afraid she would be found out and transported and he would share her fate, so he turned her in to the Germans. All the time she was in Dachau, she never knew her husband had betrayed her to save himself.'

Just like Harry Scott and Cletus Berry, Lindsey thought, thirty years later.

'After Anna finished her memoir and turned it over to the Memorial, an American officer came to see her. He had seen the records of OVRA that even

Italians could not see then. He was doing a, what is it called, background check on Salvatore Castellini. He went to see Anna. He thought she knew. She was living with Castellini, she had borne his child, she must know, she must have forgiven him. But she did not know.'

'Jesus!' Berry had sat quietly for a long time. 'There's no end to it, is there? No end to the filth, no end to the betrayals.'

Pacinelli stared, then said, 'Please, *signore*, I beg you to not give up hope. Let me, at least, keep my hope.'

Businesslike, Lindsey asked, 'What did she do?'

Pacinelli whispered his reply. 'She took her own life.'

There was silence at the table, then Berry raised his face. To Lindsey it was as if a mask had descended over his features. 'First place I'd look for the chariot would be in that catacomb.'

Every head turned toward him.

'Simple police work,' Berry said. 'You're looking for something, you don't know where it is, you start with the last place you knew where it was and work from there. Just the way your mother would say, 'Well, where did you have it last?' when you lose something.'

A little later, as Lindsey and Berry were preparing to leave, Sara Lazarini excused herself for a few minutes. She returned carrying a cup full of coins and doled them out to Lindsey and Berry, half to each. 'You give these to *tsedokeh*,' she told them. '*Per carita. Capite?*'

They both nodded.

Outside in the Via del Portico d'Ottavia, waiting for a cab to carry them back to their hotel, they counted the money. The denominations were all small, and they didn't add up to any significant amount. As they were about to give up, Lindsey said, 'Wait a minute. How many coins did she give you, Petrus? Not their value — how many actual coins?' Even as he spoke, he was counting his own collection of Italian coins. There were eighteen of them.

Berry counted his and said, 'Eighteen.'

* * *

Thirty-six hours after hearing Mosé Lazarini and Carlo Pacinelli's story in the house on the Via del Portico d'Ottavia, Lindsey and Berry were climbing down a wooden staircase beneath the sub-basement of the Grand Temple on the Lungotevere de Cenci. With them was Carlo Pacinelli, temporarily resuming his long-outgrown role as beadle of the temple.

Lindsey had spent the day working on his report, transmitting it to Desmond Richelieu in Colorado, and at Richelieu's urging, to Detective Marcie Sokolov at Midtown North in New York. He even purchased a handful of Villa del Parco postcards and a sheet of Italian postage stamps, and dispatched greetings to the States: to Anna Maria Berry; to his mother and her new husband, Gordon Sloane; to the Coffman family; and to his old friend Mathilde Wilbur at her home in Oakland.

Then he turned another card picture-side down and held his pen poised over the message area. He settled for scribbling a generic greeting on the card and addressing it to Jamie Wilkerson. Marvia would see it, her new husband would see it, and they would decide what to make of it.

★ ★ ★

Lindsey, Berry, and Carlo Pacinelli were dressed in warm quilted jackets, heavy shoes and thick socks, and woolen gloves. Unlike the catacombs of the early Christians, which had become religious shrines and tourist attractions for visitors to Rome, the Jewish catacombs — these, at least — were seldom visited. The floor was hard-packed dirt. The ceiling was low. They were armed with a few simple tools: a crowbar, a hammer, a screw-driver, a roll of bubble-wrap, and a roll of duct tape. There was no installed lighting; instead two of them carried flashlights while the third carried the tools. A claustrophobic chill ran through Lindsey. A shift of the earth, a minor cave-in, and they would be lost, buried like characters in a Poe story.

No holy relics here. The catacombs had

become storage rooms for old records and files, abandoned equipment, and broken furniture. Why didn't they just throw it away? Far from being exotic, the catacombs could have been a storage vault beneath Midtown North or SPUDS Central in Denver.

Lindsey and Berry had taken breakfast at the Villa del Parco. Berry had become quieter since leaving New York, as if he had parted from his home territory and was uncomfortable, tentative in his new surroundings. And, Lindsey knew, he'd left his revolver in Zaffira Fornari's New York apartment. Desmond Richelieu's pull might get him a passport and a plane ticket in record time, but it would not get a firearm onto that jetliner.

They passed a pile of cracked pews, obviously long since replaced in the temple and abandoned beneath the earth. Somewhere nearby, Lindsey realized, the Tiber flowed. Some formation of rock and soil kept the catacombs dry despite the proximity of the river.

And there it was: a gray tarpaulin, a layer of dust, square corners protruding.

It could have been a box of file folders, it could have been a case of wine bottles, but Lindsey knew. Somehow, they all knew.

'So many years,' Pacinelli said.

None of them reached to pull back the tarp.

'I never looked for it. I did not. It is so strange. Was I the only one who knew? And I never thought to search. I wanted to know, only to know. To learn and to teach. This is it, you think?'

Petrus Berry said, 'I think.'

Lindsey said, 'You remove the tarpaulin, Petrus. He was your brother. You have the right to do it.'

Berry lifted away the heavy gray canvas. Beneath it lay a simple wooden box. No fancy casket of polished wood and metal; just an ordinary rough packing crate. Stenciled on the side, the figures faint and faded after more than fifty years, was only the number 18.

Berry held out his hand and Lindsey placed the crowbar in it. Berry slid the wedge-shaped end of the crowbar under the lid. He leaned on the other end and a half-century-old nail screamed and yielded. He moved the wedge-end a few inches and pried again, then again, and then the top of the crate was upraised at an oblique angle.

Lindsey exhaled loudly. He realized he'd been holding his breath.

Berry dropped the crowbar at his feet with a soft thump. He grasped the edge of the crate with one gloved hand, the edge of the lid with the other, and pulled the lid upright.

The catacombs were sealed off from any natural light. The only light was provided by Lindsey's and Pacinelli's flashlights. Their feet had stirred up long-still dust particles, and their flashlight beams cast cones of reflected light.

Lindsey and Carlo Pacinelli both leaned forward, pointing their flashlights into the packing crate. All that was visible was a layer of sawdust. Berry plunged his hands into it and shoveled sawdust out of the crate, onto the dirt floor of the catacomb. He gestured with his head to Lindsey, not speaking.

Lindsey understood. He handed his

flashlight to Pacinelli and pitched in with the task. He felt an unidentifiable shape, worked his hands lower, and felt a solid, squared-off corner.

Lindsey and Berry made eye contact. Simultaneously they lifted.

Pacinelli stepped back, playing both flashlights on the chariot as Lindsey and Berry lifted it. Lindsey ended his eye contact with Berry, looking down at the ancient toy. It was covered with a thin chamois sack. Lindsey and Berry worked it carefully out of its protective covering.

The black horse and the white, the silver-work, the perfect miniature wheels with their spokes of ancient wood. What would William Van Huysen think of this! The Hebrew letters *chet yod* were still visible, worked into the Silver Chariot. A dark stain marked one sharp corner of the dark marble base.

The explosion that echoed through the catacombs couldn't possibly be as loud as it sounded, but Carlo Pacinelli screamed and Lindsey and Berry turned to find the source of the sound. A second shot followed the first. Lindsey saw the muzzle flash and in that instant he was certain that he and Berry acted as a single organism controlled by a single nervous system. They swung the chariot forward, released it, waited for what could only have been a fraction of a second but seemed like an endless, frozen moment in eternity, then heard the sickening crunch of bone as the chariot struck a human being directly in the face.

Carlo Pacinelli lay on the earth. He was moaning so he must be alive. He had dropped both flashlights. One had gone out, its lens and bulb smashed, but the other lay on the earth, still sending a beam of light through the stale, newly disturbed, dust-laden air.

Berry got to it first. He shined it on the gunman as Lindsey knelt beside him. The heavy chariot base had crushed his face. The bland features, the whole nondescript, unremarkable face, was a hopeless, bloody ruin. There was a deep indentation dead center on the pale forehead, precisely where the bullet had entered Cletus Berry's forehead in the alley in

Hell's Kitchen. Lindsey laid his fingers on the side of the man's throat, searching for a pulse, knowing there would be none, then knowing he was right.

The chariot had landed right side up and apparently undamaged. Lindsey grinned at that, knowing how incongruous his reaction was. 'Look after Pacinelli, Petrus. This one is dead.'

Berry turned away. Lindsey followed the beam of light from his flashlight. They bent over Pacinelli and Lindsey looked at his wound. Apparently the first bullet had struck him in the shoulder. The second had missed altogether.

'I don't think we should move him,' Berry said. 'We can't leave him here alone. One of us has to go for help, and there's only one flashlight working. Damn, damn. Okay, Hobart, you go. Take the light. Get back here fast with help. Fast!'

Lindsey took the functioning flashlight from Berry and headed back toward the stairs and the sub-basement of the Grand Temple. Before he reached the stairs, he heard Berry ask, 'You recognize the shooter, Hobart?'

'Yes,' Lindsey replied. 'Fellow named Morris Zissler. I didn't even know he was in Italy.'

24

One thing about flying on Christmas: it's the lightest travel day of the year, especially on international flights. Lindsey and Berry were able to stretch out, take all the snacks they wanted, get all the attention they wanted from the flight attendants, and act like a couple of big shots.

Lindsey was working on his report to Desmond Richelieu. Berry was reading a novel that he'd picked up at the terminal outside Rome. The sparse scattering of other passengers in the big jet seemed unanimously committed to ignoring the wholesome family movie that the airline had kindly provided for holiday viewing.

Outside the jet's windows — Lindsey's eyes were aching and he was relieved to drag them away from his monitor screen before they went on strike — he could see the Atlantic Ocean almost 40,000 feet below. The sound of a sixties song rang with perfect accuracy in Lindsey's mind's ear. *Eight miles high* . . . He could hear the guitars and the voices. His onetime schoolmate Artemis Janson would know whose song that was. Artie Janson had turned up at the wedding of Lindsey's mother and Gordon Sloane, the first time he'd seen her in a quarter-century. There had a been a momentary flash of energy between them, and then Artie was gone and Lindsey was gone and he wondered now if he would see her again, in another quarter-century.

Lindsey drew a deep breath. Berry marked his place in his book with his finger and looked at him. 'You all right, Hobart?'

'I'm okay.' Lindsey folded down the screen of his laptop. 'Just tired. It's been a hell of a case, Petrus.'

'That it has.' There was a silence, then he said, 'How are you going to treat Cletus, Hobart?'

'I want to be as kind as I can.'

'I know. He was your friend.'

'He was your brother.'

'But — '

Lindsey pursed his lips. 'But, indeed. I have to tell the truth, Petrus.'

'I'm thinking of Ester. And of Anna Maria.'

'I don't think this will change anything. I don't see how International Surety could cancel Cletus's life policy.'

'You don't?' Berry lifted his eyebrows. Lindsey didn't answer. 'No line-of-duty clause there?' Berry asked. 'No moral turpitude, no cancellation because he died in the act of committing a felony?'

Lindsey shook his head. 'Cletus was never convicted of anything, and now he can't be. You know we don't conduct posthumous trials. Besides . . . ' He let the sentence lapse and raised his eyes. Black ocean beneath, black sky above. But here where no city lights outshone them, a billion billion stars and galaxies filled the sky.

'Besides, we don't really know,' Lindsey resumed. 'Maybe Frankie Fulton was the intended victim, back in that alley. Maybe Cletus tried to come to the rescue and — well, you know the drill.'

Berry's face was drawn. 'You're trying

to be charitable, but I can't buy that. Two plus two makes four, we can't change it.' He leaned forward and slipped the paperback book into the seat pocket in front of him. 'I can't concentrate. Let the next person who sits here find it.' He shifted in his seat. 'You're right,' he went on, 'there's no way they can bring Cletus to trial and there's nothing really they can do to him. That life policy will be a big help for Ester and Anna Maria. I wouldn't be surprised, though, if the feds don't slap a tax deficiency on the estate. Maybe even try and seize his bank account, IS stock, anything else he owned. What a mess.'

Lindsey grunted.

'It's still a blow, Hobart.' Berry's forehead was furrowed. 'I never thought he'd turn out to be dirty. My own brother.'

'That hasn't been proved. We don't know for sure that he knew where the chariot was.'

Berry smiled ruefully. 'He knew. That's what Castellini was trying to get out of him. What a joke. Carlo Pacinelli could have turned it up for him. The whole thing went back to Castellini's own parents, back to the World's Fair and the *Fior di Rimini*. My guess is that Cletus and Castellini were playing a chess game over the chariot. Cletus overplayed his pieces. Castellini got little Frankie Fulton to bring him to a showdown meeting, and things got out of hand. I can't imagine Castellini wanting to kill Cletus. If he knew where the chariot was and Castellini killed him — stupid.' He shook his head.

Lindsey said, 'I think it was Castellini who overplayed his pieces. He didn't pull the trigger. Johnny Thieu Ng was the trigger man. The way I figure it, Fulton was supposed to be an example. Castellini hired Ng to kill Fulton. Ng got carried away and killed Cletus too. See what a productive worker I am, two hits for the price of one. Castellini got so angry that he had Ng killed, and Ng's buddy Bilbo Sax for good measure. And all the other people who've died for that damn toy. All the way back to Millicent Martin, who shouldn't have started hanging around with a reporter. All the way back to Massimo di Verolini.' He leaned his head on his hand.

'It all stinks, Hobart.' Berry sighed. 'So the Italian government gets the toy back and it goes into a museum, I suppose.'

Lindsey nodded. 'I suppose.'

'Professor Pacinelli gets to play the hero, and your company — you think they'll get their money back?'

Lindsey managed a faint grin. 'We'll ask for it, the Italians will date-stamp the claim, we won't hear for six months . . . It'll be fun. You know how many years it took International Surety to pay the original claim? It'll take that long for the Italian government even to look at our request for reimbursement. They'll probably pay it in current lire, which will be enough money to buy Desmond Richelieu a good Italian dinner at the best spaghetti house in Denver.'

He latched up his laptop and slid it under the seat in front of him. He'd done all the work he was going to do on this flight. He could finish when he reached New York, or even Denver. 'What I want to see,' he said, 'is what's going to happen back in New York. I know that Richelieu talked to Corporate and got Harry Scott summoned back to headquarters for a face-to-face, and Scott and his *bella signora* seem to have taken a disappearing powder.'

Berry smiled. 'I haven't heard that expression in thirty years.'

'Do I get in the old guys' club?'

'Don't ask me. I didn't even know I was old until my brother died. Then all of a sudden I felt old, Hobart.'

'I'm sorry. I didn't mean to joke.'

'That's okay. I've got to get back and do what I can for Cletus's women, that's all. But what *is* going to happen? If Giobbe were still alive, it would be different.'

'Giobbe?'

'Zaffira's husband. I asked Cletus about him once. He said it was Italian for Job.'

The flight attendant arrived with their coffee. They took the cups and thanked her. She headed for the back of the plane. Lindsey hoped that she would have some time off after they reached New York. 'I spoke with Marcie Sokolov while you were packing,' he said. 'She wants to talk to us when we get in. Mainly to me. But I think she has a kind of crush on you, Petrus, for the way you took out Merle Oates.'

'I don't like to kill anyone. I don't care what kind of thug he was.'

'Even so.'

'What about Alcide Palmiro Castellini, Hobart? We keep coming back to him, and he keeps sliding away.'

'Sokolov wouldn't say much on the phone, but it looks as if she's after him. NYPD is trying to get the feds involved. Try and make a John Gotti case out of it. Maybe even try and get up a RICO proceeding. If they can get Cele Johnston to help them, they might have a chance.'

Berry grunted and sipped his coffee. 'You think she'll buy into that?'

'I don't think Cele Johnston will go for it for a minute. Give up her fancy frou-frou antique business on Fifty-seventh Street to take a cover job as an office manager? Not a chance.'

'But if she testifies openly and doesn't go into the program . . . ' Berry left the sentence there. He didn't have to complete it.

'Funny thing is,' Lindsey said, 'Castellini tried to recruit me into his operation. He knew I was SPUDS, knew I'd worked with Cletus. He figured I knew where the chariot was, or at least that I'd find it. If he was in with Harry Scott and Moe Zissler — what a bunch, what a bunch! If I wouldn't find the toy and fetch it for him, he'd let me find it for myself, then have Scott or Zissler retrieve it for him. Scott funked it, Zissler screwed up, no chariot for Castellini.'

'Are you sure Zissler was working for Castellini?' Berry asked. 'Scott was involved, that's pretty obvious. But do you think Zissler was a freelance? You think he followed you around, Hobart, and decided he'd just make a pre-emptive strike and grab the chariot for himself?'

Lindsey sighed. 'I don't think he was smart enough for that. I think he was just another Castellini pawn. Maybe he was supposed to report in and take his orders from Harry Scott. I kind of think that was the plan. You know, Petrus, we became quite a team, didn't we?'

'That we did.' Berry nodded. 'That we did.'

Lindsey toyed with his empty coffee cup and considered asking the attendant for a refill. No, he'd wait to get something better when they reached New York. This time there would be no Morris Zissler to pick them up in his white Buick. Detective Marcie Sokolov had arranged a ride in a police cruiser from the airport into Manhattan.

'I think they'll get Castellini, but it won't be fast and it won't be easy,' Lindsey said. 'It'll probably take as long to get Castellini as it will to get the insurance money back from the Italian government. And as for Castellini's pal Randolph Amoroso . . . at least he doesn't get his magic talisman. I don't know if that will stop him from getting into the Senate, but it just might. And Oliver Shea can go to Washington and try and do some good. Let him pretend to be Jimmy Stewart.'

Berry said, 'All politics stinks, Hobart.'

★ ★ ★

The plane landed as dawn broke to the east. But once the jet dipped below the cloud layer, Lindsey saw that it was snowing again. They'd left Rome late in the afternoon of Christmas Day, and they were landing in New York early on the morning of the day after Christmas.

Officer Gulbenkian met them at the mouth of the jetway, hustled them through customs, and got them back to Zaffira Fornari's brownstone flat. Gulbenkian said that Lieutenant Sokolov had told him to stay with them until they'd rested up, then escort them to Midtown North.

Berry said, 'That's just fine with me. I'm headed for a shower and bed.'

Lindsey nodded. They'd both dropped their flight bags in the vestibule and he realized that he didn't want that second cup of coffee or anything else to eat or drink. He felt tired and stale and desperately in need of hot soapy water and a shave, and then a soft bed.

★　★　★

Lindsey knew that he and Berry weren't prisoners or even suspects. They'd been through that in Rome; the *poliziotti* and the *intendatore* and the *console americano* and the Italian *avocatto* that the *console* had got for them had dealt with that. Things had looked hairy for a little while. Harry Scott, of all people, had seemed more of an obstruction than an asset.

That was before the messages began zipping back and forth between the American consulate and the embassy in Rome, Marcie Sokolov at NYPD, the US Customs Service, the Italian government, and last but not least International Surety. Not IS in the United States, not SPUDS, but International Surety/World Headquarters.

It was classic, Lindsey thought. Desmond Richelieu hadn't got the right scoop on Harry Scott — or the complete scoop, anyway. Scott and his *bella signora* had disappeared, okay, but not before Scott gave up Alcide Castellini in exchange for a get-out-of-jail-free card for himself and his gorgeous Italian wife. They weren't part of the US Marshall's witness protection program, either. They were gone, living the good life in ... Lindsey was never able to find out through official channels, but if you asked him if he'd got a little help from his friend Anna Maria Berry, he would probably change the subject before answering.

Lindsey and Berry were sitting opposite Marcie Sokolov now. The few wreaths and Christmas streamers that had brightened Manhattan North had disappeared in whatever black hole such decorations return to every winter. Sokolov asked Lindsey, 'Don't you think Agatha Christie would have loved this? The old least-likely-suspect theory. At first I really did think that Cletus Berry's murder was a random killing, or at most that he'd gotten mixed up with the wrong crowd and was killed for his trouble. After a while you convinced me that Alcide

Castellini was involved.'

'Have you arrested him?'

'The feds have. They're doing the mambo over his art smuggling racket.'

'That's swell.' Lindsey heard the bitterness in his own voice. 'What about the killings?'

Sokolov chewed her lip. 'We're working with the feds. This is going to turn into the biggest thing since John Gotti finally went down. Castellini is standing up to his neck in a sludge pit right now, and the customs fellas and the DA's people are just throwing more and more of it at him, a bucket at a time. The only one who might have saved him was his buddy Randolph Amoroso, and he's running away from Castellini just as fast as his shapely little legs can carry him. Not that it's going to save him. The party bosses are scared now, and *they're* running away from *him*, and that makes it look like a free trip to Washington for Oliver Shea.'

'That's politics for you,' Berry said.

'I just can't understand Moe Zissler,' Lindsey said, shaking his head.

'Why not, Lindsey? Because he worked

for your precious International Surety corporation?' Berry made an angry hissing sound. 'So did Cletus.'

'I know.' Lindsey nodded sadly. 'You just think that a crook is some guy wearing a black shirt and a yellow tie.' Then to Sokolov: 'Did you find out what happened to Benjamino Bermudez?'

'My partner Roland Roscoe took that question on while you fellers were out of town. He went right along with your theory, Lindsey. Castellini was getting panicky after Cletus Berry's death. That was supposed to be a quiet little misfortune. There was too much fuss being raised. Largely by you, I should add.' She tapped Lindsey's sleeve with a startling, scarlet-painted fingernail. 'He had to get up to Berry's nest and vacuum the files. He was familiar enough in the Torrington to get in at night, but he couldn't have poor Mino telling us he was there. So . . . ' She made a toy gun of her hand and pointed it at Lindsey. 'Pow!' She grinned. 'For once he pulled the trigger himself. It's going to be a bitch to prove it, but that's the one that will make

Miss Marcie a happy little she-dick.'

'Pinning a Castellini to the wall is almost fun, isn't it?' Berry said.

'You bet it is.' Her telephone made a peculiar sound and she picked it up and murmured into it. She put it down and said, 'Look, this is going to take months to clean up. Maybe years. We have a permanent address for both of you?' Without waiting for an answer she opened a manila folder, nodded, then laid it down. She looked from Lindsey to Berry and back. 'Pinopolis, South Carolina? Denver?'

'I may stay in New York,' Berry said. 'I've got my pension and my Social Security. Anna Maria's my only kin. If Zaffira moves in with Ester and Anna Maria, maybe I can get her place. Permanently. I want to be near that little girl. I can't replace her daddy, but at least she'll have an uncle.'

'Okay. Good. Lindsey?'

'I'm headed back. If you don't need me, I'll be on the first flight I can get.'

'Long as we can reach you.'

Lindsey got halfway out of his chair,

then slid back down. 'One other thing.'

Sokolov raised her eyebrows.

'Castellini and his, ah, associates didn't mind killing people. I've worked on murder cases before, even cases where there was more than one murder. But I've never been involved in one where they just keep killing and killing.'

Sokolov and Petrus Berry waited.

'Why,' Lindsey asked, 'didn't Castellini have me killed before I ever left for Italy? I was getting into his plans; I was stirring things up and making trouble for him. And he didn't mind having people killed.'

Sokolov said, 'I'm sorry, Lindsey, if this hurts your ego. But you were just a pimple. Alcide Castellini could have popped you any time, but then you might have gotten infected. You understand what I'm saying? This case only blew up on him to start with because he took Cletus Berry out, or had him taken out. Then your company sent you in. I know who your boss is. I know about Desmond Richelieu. And so does Alcide Castellini. Castellini might not have been afraid of the NYPD, but he didn't want to take on

Desmond Richelieu. If Castellini took you out he'd have Richelieu himself to contend with. He figured it was easier to leave you in place than to deal with somebody tougher.'

Lindsey stood up. Berry hesitated, then did the same. Lindsey shook hands with Marcie Sokolov, waited while Berry did so, then turned and started away from Sokolov's desk. Then he turned back. 'That's what Castellini thought, is it?'

'That's my guess.'

'That doesn't hurt my ego. Castellini's in jail now. He's — how did you put it so elegantly? — neck-deep in sludge. And I am going home.'

25

Lindsey booked his own flight back to Denver. He didn't have much packing to do. Some paperwork at Midtown North, and some more at the US Attorney's office. He was starting to feel as if he and Berry were the Hardy Boys.

He had walked into a family shattered by violence and grief and helped them to find a degree of peace and hope of justice. But that was tempered by the dawning realization that Cletus Berry, *pater familias*, had been dirty for most of the past two decades. Faithful husband, loving father, dear brother . . . criminal.

It was strange, Lindsey thought, how he had taken to New York. As apprehensive as he'd been before his arrival, he'd found its astonishing dynamism a challenge and then a pleasure. And the great city had lived up to its promise as a town with a heart. Trouble was, to find it you had to peel away the layers of anger and filth. He'd succeeded, but now he was going home.

Petrus Berry proposed a farewell dinner. Lindsey agreed and suggested that Ester, Zaffira, and Anna Maria be included in the invitation. International Surety would pick up the tab.

They were assembled in the 73rd Street apartment. Anna wore a Rangers jersey and jeans. She held little Ezio on her lap. Ester and Zaffira, still in black, the mirrors and pictures on their walls still covered, declined.

'But Anna Maria should go,' Ester urged. 'She needs to live.'

'You too, *sorella, shvester*.' Zaffira touched her sister's cheek.

Ester shivered visibly. 'Anna Maria, go with your uncle and Mr. Lindsey. Try to enjoy your dinner.'

Anna put her dog on the floor. 'Can I bring my friend Shoshana?'

Ester looked to Lindsey. 'Of course,' he said.

Anna headed for her room. Almost at once Lindsey heard the clicking of the computer keyboard. When she emerged she had worked a magic trick, changing her clothing in an instant to a pale button-down shirt, plaid woolen skirt, and black tights. She had metamorphosed into a slim, vibrant woman of twenty. The brilliant mind that shone from her eyes was equaled only by her olive beauty.

She crossed the living room to Ester's side. Ester folded her black-clad arms around her. 'Shoshana says she can come but her mom says we have to eat at her dad's restaurant. She'll meet us downstairs.' To the two men she said, 'You'll like it. It's a real New York place.'

Lindsey blinked and she was a little girl again. She had reached inside of him and grasped his heart in her small hands. He realized that he had fallen in father-love with this child. That was the story of his life. Whoever he loved, he lost.

★   ★   ★

Shoshana was a lighter-skinned version of Anna. Lindsey and Berry and the girls caught a cab on Lexington Avenue and headed downtown through slush-filled streets to Pete's Tavern.

By the time they reached the low 50s, Anna put her hand on Lindsey's sleeve. 'Tell me about my cousin Mosé. And Abramo and Sara, my aunt and uncle. But mainly I want to know about Mosé.'

Lindsey looked at Berry, who nodded. 'Abramo and Sara. They seem much older than your mother or your Aunt Zaffira. Sara speaks this wonderful language all her own — Yiddish and Italian and Hebrew and English all mixed together. And your uncle is a quiet man. Serious. They were very kind to Petrus and me.'

'What about Mosé?'

'He's a lot like you. Smart. He's interested in history.'

'I know that.'

'But I think he's more interested in the future. He cares about the past, but . . . he's just a little boy, Anna Maria.'

'I know that.'

'Well, then.' Lindsey didn't know what else to say.

'Girls mature faster than boys,' Anna

said. Her friend Shoshana nodded in agreement. Lindsey thought, *You bet they do.*

'I want to visit him,' Anna resumed. 'My cousin and my other relatives. I want to go to Italy and Israel and Africa. I'm African too, and I want to find where my black ancestors came from.'

Lindsey inhaled. 'I think that would be a very good idea.'

The cab pulled up at the restaurant. Lindsey paid the fare and made a note for his expense account. They made their way into the warm, noisy restaurant. The girls ran into the kitchen to visit Shoshana's dad. The place was dark and felt old. Polished wood and polished brass. Well-heeled, comfortable clientele. Had Victor Hopkins and Millicent Martinelli shared a romantic dinner here before she wound up with duct tape over her mouth and nose?

Lindsey and Berry settled at a white linen-topped table. They ordered only ice water. Before long the two girls strode back from the kitchen, not squealing children but young princesses, aware of the power they were coming into and reveling in it.

Berry signaled the waiter and asked for menus for four, but the waiter said it was taken care of.

Soon the food arrived. A steak for Lindsey and another for Berry. The girls had pasta with seafood. Not kosher, but if Shoshana's father was the chef here then the families must have reached an accommodation with the world.

Shoshana said, 'My dad is one of the top chefs in the whole city. There was an article about him in *New York*.'

Something made Lindsey look up. He was facing the street entrance of the restaurant, his back to the kitchen. Between him and the street door, dining with their heads close together, sat Alcide Palmiro Castellini his flunky Campana, and the nameless woman who had greeted Lindsey at the Stanford White house.

Lindsey froze. Had they been there all along? Or had Castellini and company arrived after Lindsey and Berry were seated at their own table, while the girls were visiting in the kitchen? Whichever it was, he should have been on the alert. The restaurant was within whistling distance of Gramercy Park. Somehow Lindsey had expected that Castellini would dine at home, especially under the circumstances, but obviously he'd been wrong on that count.

Castellini wore another of his elegantly tailored suits. His perfectly groomed hair caught the soft light of the old-fashioned fixtures. He lifted a glass of red wine and across the rim he made eye contact with Lindsey.

Lindsey turned back to his own party. The girls demanded a recounting of Lindsey and Berry's adventure in Rome. Lindsey had answered Anna's questions in the cab, but she pressed him for details.

He did his best, and handed off half the questions to Berry. Anna couldn't hear enough about her cousin Mosé and his parents. She wanted to learn everything about *Professore* Pacinelli and was fascinated by the Jewish catacombs beneath the Grand Temple.

Lindsey glanced up, checking the Castellini table often. Castellini sat at a right angle to the front door. He could swivel his head ninety degrees and see the entrance to the restaurant or Lindsey and his companions. Lindsey hoped that the two girls would leave the table again, and finally they did, just before dessert was served, to visit Shoshana's father.

As soon as they were out of sight, Lindsey leaned forward and told Berry that Castellini and associates were a few tables away. Berry nodded and answered in a low rumble, 'Of course. They got here same time as the breadsticks.'

Lindsey had another glimpse of Castellini, then looked beyond him. The glass and brass front doors of the tavern were steamed against the cold Manhattan night. Even so, Lindsey could see the tell-tale police cruiser flashers outside. The steamed doors swung open to admit a party of men and women, some in uniform. Two uniformed New York City cops stationed themselves in the doorway. As the newcomers in civilian clothes moved into the restaurant, Lindsey recognized Marcie Sokolov and her partner. There was a look of intense excitement on her face.

Campana started from his chair. One hand moved toward his shoulder. At the same moment Lindsey sensed Berry tensing, reaching toward his own shoulder. But Castellini grabbed Campana's wrist and pulled him back into his seat.

They made a frozen tableau, then Campana lowered his hands slowly to the white tablecloth. Castellini and their young woman companion did the same. Lindsey could see Castellini nod slightly and mouth something that looked like, 'All right, then.'

Under Marcie Sokolov's direction, uniformed officers brought Castellini's party to their feet. They removed weapons from all three. The woman even had a small revolver in her purse.

'Could have been very difficult,' Berry said. 'You have to make the suspect aware that resistance is futile before he does something foolish and nasty. You don't want a shoot-out, especially in a crowd.'

In minutes Sokolov and the cops and

Castellini and his pals were gone.

Anna and Shoshana returned from the kitchen. They'd missed the excitement. The room full of *blasé* New Yorkers went on eating and drinking.

* * *

Desmond Richelieu said, 'This is a hell of a thing, Lindsey.' The sunlight glinted off his gold-rimmed glasses.

'We found the chariot,' Lindsey said, 'and the company is entitled to get its money back.' He paused. 'If we're not in any hurry.'

Richelieu swung around in his swivel chair and gazed up at the portrait of J. Edgar Hoover. When he swung back his head drooped. 'The chief in a dress,' he whispered. 'In a dress.' To Lindsey he said, 'You've done it again, buster. I send you on a straightforward assignment and you land up to your neck in crazy complications.'

Lindsey spread his hands. 'You want me to go back to paying for fender-benders? Why did you shanghai me into

SPUDS? You knew what you were getting.'

'New York SPUDS is in trouble,' Richelieu said. 'We're in trouble. Harry Scott was a shock, but that's IS International's problem. And Morris Zissler — who'd have thought it?'

'Not me,' Lindsey admitted. 'I didn't think he had the brains to brown-bag a lunch and claim a fancy meal on his expense account.'

Richelieu smiled ruefully. 'But Cletus Berry! He was one of my own. We were family. I sent you to nail the bastard who killed a member of my family, Lindsey, and you discovered that he was dirty. I can't get over it.' He stood and strode to the window, then gazed down at the stream and the grassy park outside IS's suite in the Denver high-rise. There was a January thaw in the air. The ice clogging the stream had broken up and the fresh water was flowing again. The snow had melted enough to show patches of green against the white. One thing about Denver snow, it stayed a lot cleaner than New York snow.

Richelieu spun on his heel. 'Lindsey,' he barked, 'how would you like to go put New York back together for me?'

Petrus and Anna Maria Berry were in New York. It was something to think about. Marcie Sokolov was in New York.

Lindsey did not feel compelled to answer at once.

We do hope that you have enjoyed reading this large print book.

Did you know that all of our titles are available for purchase?

We publish a wide range of high quality large print books including:
Romances, Mysteries, Classics
General Fiction
Non Fiction and Westerns

Special interest titles available in large print are:
The Little Oxford Dictionary
Music Book, Song Book
Hymn Book, Service Book

Also available from us courtesy of Oxford University Press:
Young Readers' Dictionary
(large print edition)
Young Readers' Thesaurus
(large print edition)

For further information or a free brochure, please contact us at:
Ulverscroft Large Print Books Ltd.,
The Green, Bradgate Road, Anstey,
Leicester, LE7 7FU, England.
Tel: (00 44) **0116 236 4325**
Fax: (00 44) **0116 234 0205**

Other titles in the
Linford Mystery Library:

THE SEPIA SIREN KILLER

Richard A. Lupoff

Prior to World War II, black actors were restricted to minor roles in mainstream films — though there was a 'black' Hollywood that created films with all-black casts for exhibition to black audiences. When a cache of long-lost films is discovered by cinema researchers, the aged director Edward 'Speedy' MacReedy appears to reclaim his place in film history. But insurance investigator Hobart Lindsey and homicide officer Marvia Plum soon find themselves enmeshed in a frightening web of arson and murder with its roots deep in the tragic events of a past era . . .

KILLING COUSINS

Fletcher Flora

Suburban housewife Willie Hogan is selfish, bored, and beautiful, passing her time at the country club and having casual affairs. Her husband Howard doesn't seem to care particularly — until one night she comes home from a party to discover he has packed his things and intends to leave her for good. Panicked, Willie grabs Howard's gun and shoots him dead. With the help of her current paramour, Howard's clever cousin Quincy, the body is disposed of — but unbeknownst to either of them, their problems are only just beginning . . .

A CORNISH VENGEANCE

Rena George

Silas Venning, millionaire owner of a
luxury yacht company, is found
hanged in a remote Cornish wood. It
looks like suicide — but his widow,
celebrated artist Laura Anstey, doesn't
think so. She enlists Loveday Ross to
help prove her suspicions. But there
can be no doubts about the killing of
Venning's former employee Brian
Penrose — not when he's mown down
by a hit-and-run driver right in front
of Loveday's boyfriend, DI Sam Kitto.
Could they be dealing with *two*
murders?

THE COVER GIRL KILLER

Richard A. Lupoff

When a chartered helicopter plunges into the icy waters of Lake Tahoe, killing its millionaire passenger, what seems a routine claim against a life insurance policy turns into a complex mystery for investigator Hobart Lindsey and his policewoman girlfriend Marvia Plum — for the multimillion-dollar policy is to go an unnamed model who posed for the cover of an ephemeral mystery paperback in 1951. Lindsey's own life is in danger as he tries to find the now-aged model (if she's still alive!), on a trail full of murder and deception . . .

MURDER DOWN EAST

Victor Rousseau

Rich spinster Abbie Starr dies in her mansion without leaving a will. Her fortune is thought to have been converted into securities that have been hidden in the mansion — but searches there fail to find anything except a big overdraft. The courts give what is left to cousins Jenny Starr and Elsie Garry, allowing them to run the mansion as a boarding house. But when Jenny is found murdered, the evidence points to Elsie as the killer . . .